ROWAN

AND THE

KEEPER OF THE CRYSTAL

The Crystal dims.
The Chooser is summoned ...

When the man from the distant land of Maris delivers his mysterious message to the people of Rin, Rowan is shocked to discover what it means to him. Within hours he is travelling far from home, all the way to the glittering sea, and into the strange world of the Maris people.

There, caught up in mystery and intrigue, Rowan must try to fulfil an ancient promise. But who can he trust? And is he brave enough to face the terrors ahead?

The Rowan series

Rowan of Rin
Rowan and the Travellers
Rowan and the Keeper of the Crystal
Rowan and the Zebak
Rowan of the Bukshah

ROWAN

AND THE
KEEPER OF THE CRYSTAL

ANTH ONY

EMILY RODDA

An Omnibus Book from Scholastic Australia

For all the children
who asked for more about Rowan

LEXILE™ 600

Omnibus Books
52 Fullarton Road, Norwood SA 5067
an imprint of Scholastic Australia Pty Ltd (ABN 11 000 614 577)
PO Box 579, Gosford NSW 2250.
www.scholastic.com.au

Part of the Scholastic Group
Sydney · Auckland · New York · Toronto · London · Mexico City ·
New Delhi · Hong Kong · Buenos Aires · Puerto Rico

First published in 1996.
Reprinted in 1996, 1997 (three times), 1999,
2000, 2001 (twice), 2002.
First published in this edition in 2003.
Reprinted in 2003 (three times).
Text copyright © Emily Rodda, 1996.
Cover artwork copyright © Barry Downard, 2003.
Maps copyright © Omnibus Books, 2003.

National Library of Australia Cataloguing-in-Publication entry
Rodda, Emily, 1948–   .
Rowan and the keeper of the crystal.
Rev. ed.
For children aged 9–12 years.
ISBN 1 86291 537 7.
1. Rowan (Fictitious character: Rodda)—Juvenile fiction.
2. Courage—Juvenile fiction. I. Title. (Series: Rowan series; 3).
A823.3

Typeset in 13/15 pt Garamond 3 by Clinton Ellicott, Adelaide.
Printed in Australia by Griffin Press, Adelaide.

10 9 8 7 6 5 4   3 4 5 / 0

Contents

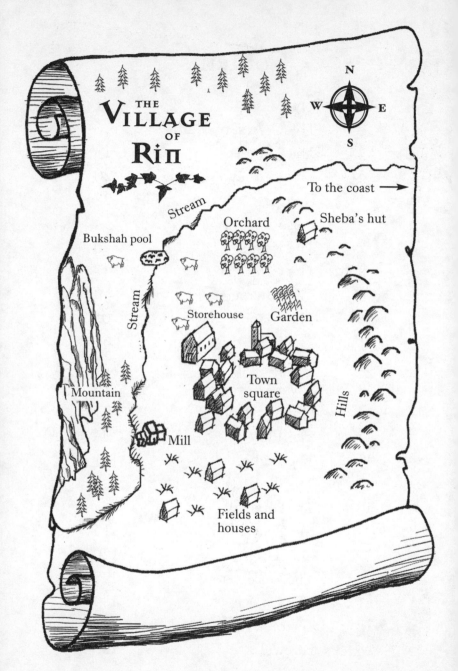

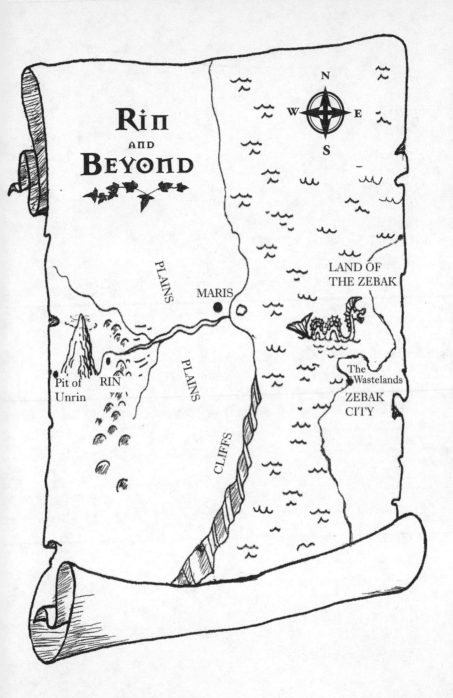

1 – The Message

even words, written in dull black ink on a thin parchment that smelt of oil and fish.

The Crystal dims. The Chooser is summoned ...

The sun was gentle on the valley of Rin, the day the message came. A faint breeze ruffled the blossoms of the hoopberry trees in the orchard.

Rowan stood by the bukshah pool, breathing in the sweet scent carried to him by the breeze. As the great beasts he tended drank, he gazed up at the snow-capped Mountain that overlooked the valley. He could hear the sounds of the birds, the insects chirruping in the grass, the people working in the vegetable gardens and the fields. He could hear the bubbling of the stream as it rippled through the village and wound away through the dreaming green hills behind him, on its journey to the sea.

For Rowan, this seemed a day like any other. And yet the messenger was already very near. He was no longer just a flicker of shining blue in the distance. Already he was almost in sight of the village as he half ran, half stumbled through the hills, following the stream like a lifeline. Already his small webbed hands were feeling inside his cloak for the parchment he carried.

In just a few moments the bell in the village square would ring, to signal his arrival, to call a meeting.

And after this day, for Rowan, nothing would ever be the same again.

* * *

Rowan joined the crowd in the square, standing on tiptoe the better to see the messenger. He had come running, like the others, when he heard the bell ring. Now he watched as Lann, the oldest person in the village, took the parchment from the fainting Maris man and read it aloud.

Seven words.

The Crystal dims. The Chooser is summoned.

Afterwards, Rowan remembered it all as though it was a dream. Lann's voice, loud in the square. Her wrinkled hand holding out the parchment. The midday sunlight filtering through the trees. The surprised, murmuring crowd.

The soft breezes and sweet scents of the valley of Rin moved about him. He was surrounded by people he had known all his life. Familiar birds sang in the trees above his head. He felt no prickle of fear, or inner warning. All he felt was interest, and pleasure, because something unexpected had happened to interrupt the routine of the day. A strange visitor, all the way from the coast, from the home of the Maris. And an even stranger message.

The Crystal dims ...

"What do you think it means?" Rowan whispered to Jiller, his mother, standing tall and straight beside him.

She didn't answer. But when he looked up at her, to ask her again, the words died on his lips. Jiller's face was drained of colour, and her eyes were fixed on the parchment in Lann's hand. Behind her, Strong Jonn of the Orchard moved to put an arm around her shoulders. His mouth was grim.

Rowan realised then that the message was of great importance. But still, he had no idea that it was something that was going to affect him.

Feeling a rising thrill of excited curiosity, he looked again at the figure crouching in exhaustion on the hard stones of the village square. It was his first glimpse of a Maris man. And none of the stories told by villagers coming home from journeys to the coast, none of the pictures he had seen in the house of books, had prepared him for the reality. He knew he shouldn't stare, but it was hard to tear his eyes away.

The man was clothed from wrist to ankle in tight-fitting blue garments that glimmered in the sunlight. Light boots covered his feet. He had cast aside the hood and gloves he had been wearing when he first staggered into the village. Now everyone could see the glistening, hairless, blue-white skin of his head, face and neck, his flat, glassy-looking eyes, his wide mouth and his small webbed hands.

He huddled, panting, at Lann's feet. She looked down at him, leaning heavily on her stick.

"What is your name, Maris man?" she asked abruptly.

"Perlain, of the clan Pandellis."

"How long since you left the coast, Perlain?"

"Four suns," gasped the man. His voice was dull and rasping, and he raised his webbed hand to his throat as he spoke, as if the words hurt him.

A murmur of surprise rose from the crowd. It took the people of Rin at least a week to travel between their valley and the coast. This man must have run much of the way, and barely slept. No wonder he was exhausted. They looked at him with new respect.

"You have made good time," said Lann. "You have done well, Perlain of Pandellis."

"There is great danger," croaked the Maris man. "The Chooser ..."

"The Chooser of Rin has heard the summons, and will obey it," Lann said calmly. "There has always been danger. But never in three hundred years have we failed to answer the call. The Chooser and the First-born will leave for the coast with you at sunset."

Rowan's heart leaped. Danger! Someone was about to go into great danger. Someone from Rin. But what was the danger? What did all this mean? Who was the Chooser? Chooser of what?

Perlain was shaking his head. "No. Not—so long. Every hour—every minute—is precious!" His throat moved as he swallowed painfully.

"You have been travelling in the sun, as well as under the moon, for too long. You must rest. You must soak. Or you will die, Perlain," said Lann.

"It does not matter." The Maris man wet his dry lips. "The death of one is—of no account."

"This is your belief, but not ours," Lann answered firmly. "And besides, our people must prepare for the journey. The Chooser will leave at sunset." She raised her voice. "Is it agreed?"

There was a moment's silence. Rowan looked up curiously into Lann's face. She was frowning, staring at someone in the crowd. Someone very near to Rowan.

He turned his head to see who it was. All around him, other children and most of the adults were doing the same thing. But a few of the adults' faces were serious and intent.

They know, he thought. *They know.*

"Is it agreed?" Lann repeated. "Does the Chooser agree?"

Rowan felt a movement as someone stepped forward to stand alone in the centre of the square.

"Yes," said a quiet voice. "I agree. We leave at sunset."

The Maris man looked eagerly towards the sound, then bowed his head, touching his forehead to the ground.

"Chooser of Rin, who holds the fate of Maris in your hands, I greet you in the name of the Keeper of the Crystal," he breathed. "I am your servant. I am the sand beneath your feet. My life is yours."

Rowan blinked, and gasped. He couldn't believe what was happening. He couldn't understand it.

This can't be right! I would have known of it. There must be some mistake, he thought wildly.

But there was no mistake.

The person accepting the reverence of the crouching Maris man, the person the message had called the Chooser, the person who was about to go into unknown peril, was Jiller, his mother.

2 – The Crystal of Maris

hat is happening? Mother, tell me!"

Rowan clutched at Jiller's arm as they hurried home from the square. But she strode on, frowning and silent.

"Wait, skinny rabbit," Strong Jonn muttered to him. He jerked his head at the chattering crowd behind them. "Your mother will not speak till we are alone. Be patient." His voice was as confident as always, but Rowan could tell by his face that he was worried and shaken.

Jonn and Jiller walked quickly on. Rowan's young sister, Annad, skipped along in front of them. Annad understood little of what had happened in the square. She and her friends had been far too busy whispering to each other and peeping at the strange-looking Maris man to pay attention to anything else.

Rowan stumbled behind, his mind whirling with questions, thoughts and fears.

All he understood so far was that his mother had to go to Maris. That he, her first-born child, had to go with her. And that some terrible danger awaited them at the end of the journey.

But what danger? And why did they have to go at all?

Maris. Rowan tried to remember all he knew about

it. Timon the teacher had told the children many tales of the land on the coast. Tales of serpents of the sea, of battles and storms—and some of the history of the strange Maris folk.

But suddenly Rowan remembered one special day under the Teaching Tree. A warm summer's day.

Timon had been showing them pictures from a book. Pictures of Maris folk. They all looked alike to Rowan, except that some wore silver, some blue, and some green.

"The Maris are a secret people," Timon had said, pointing to the pictures one by one. "Though they trade freely with us and others from across the sea, they do not open their hearts to strangers, and little is known of them.

"But some things we do know. The Maris are divided into three tribes, or clans: the silver clan of Umbray, the green clan of Fisk, the blue clan of Pandellis. In ancient times the clans fought bitterly. Every night, it is said, the sea ran with blood, and the serpents feasted on Maris flesh.

"But for a thousand years the clans have been united under one all-powerful leader—the Keeper of the Crystal. The first Keeper was a man called Orin the Wise. It was he who found the Crystal, a treasure of great power and mystery, in a cave beneath the Maris sea ..."

Rowan was tired, that day. He had been woken in the night by a bad dream, and it had taken him a long time to fall back to sleep.

So he was half drowsing under the Teaching Tree, listening to Timon with only part of his mind.

"Rowan of the Bukshah! What did I just say?"

Timon's voice jerked him wide awake.

"Ah—ah—there are three clans ..." he stammered,

feeling himself blush. "Their leader is—the Keeper of the Crystal."

The other children giggled and nudged one another. They knew how shy Rowan was. And usually he was quiet and good in lessons. They thought it was funny to see him caught out.

Timon frowned warningly at them, and went on. "Very well. Once there was a fourth clan, the clan of Mirril. They were experts in poison. They created a thousand and one deadly poisons, and for every poison, an antidote. But the Mirril were all destroyed when the Zebak invaded the coast three hundred years ago."

Again he looked at Rowan, his grey eyes piercing.

"What else happened three hundred years ago, Rowan?"

"That was when our ancestors came here, and Rin began," Rowan said in a low voice.

Timon nodded.

"Correct. The Zebak have tried to invade the coast of this land many times. But three hundred years ago they came with an army of warrior slaves chained to the oars of their ships. Those slaves were our ancestors."

Timon's face was grave as he continued.

"The morning the Zebak landed, all the Maris clans were meeting in their separate meeting houses. No one had been left outside on guard. No one knew the enemy had come. The Zebak crept up to the Mirril house and threw an exploding fire inside. There was a great roar. Sheets of flame shot up to the sky. The building fell, and burned. Everyone died. Not a single member of the Mirril clan was left alive. No man, no woman, no child."

Timon had everyone's attention now. The children

under the Teaching Tree were silent. All well knew the terror of fire.

"Our ancestors saw this happen," Timon went on. "They saw the Zebak laugh as the fire raged. The horror of that moment was one of the reasons they were roused to turn against the Zebak at last. They broke their chains and joined the people of this land to fight and defeat their enemy. It was the most important day in our history."

Then Timon did a strange thing. He closed the book, and leaned forward. And suddenly it seemed to Rowan that Timon was speaking to him alone.

"We must never forget," Timon said slowly, his eyes fixed on Rowan's, "that the Maris folk have been vital to our safety ever since. For the Maris guard the coast. Without them, the Zebak would have come and claimed us again, long ago. The Zebak plot ceaselessly against this land, and they grow more cunning with every year that passes. We must never lose the trust of the Maris, whatever the cost."

Soon afterwards, the lesson had ended. Thinking about it later, Rowan decided that he had been foolish to think that Timon was speaking particularly to him. For why should this story be more special to Rowan than it was to any of the other Rin children?

But now, the message from Maris still ringing in his ears, he felt differently.

Timon *was* speaking especially to me that day, he thought, his heart beginning to thud. Timon knew that some day the message from Maris would come. He was warning me that I must not fight it. That I must do my duty.

What duty?

It was something to do with the Crystal. The fabled Crystal of Maris.

The Crystal dims. The Chooser is summoned.

"Few outside Maris understand just how powerful and mysterious the Crystal is. Very few," Timon had said once.

And again, his grey eyes had seemed to flick in Rowan's direction.

Rowan's steps slowed. Yes. The Crystal was at the heart of this. Had Timon said anything more about it?

Just one thing. And he had said it gravely, as though it was very important.

"The Maris live long. Far longer than we of Rin. And the Keepers reach a greater age than any of them, because of the power of the Crystal. But still there comes a time when each Keeper knows death is near. At this time the Crystal begins to lose its fire and its strength. Then a new Keeper must be chosen, to take the old one's place. The new Keeper must join with the Crystal before the old Keeper dies, so that its power is not lost."

The Crystal dims ...

Rowan's throat tightened. Suddenly he saw what the message meant. Far away in Maris, the Keeper of the Crystal was dying. A new Keeper had to be chosen.

But why had the message come to Jiller? Why had the messenger called her the Chooser? What did she, a woman of Rin, have to do with the Keeper of the Crystal?

Rowan looked up and saw that Jiller and Jonn had stopped, and were waiting for him. They had reached the pathway that led into their garden and the fields beyond. Annad had run through the gate already, leaving it gaping wide.

He hurried to join them.

"Go into the house, now, Rowan," Jiller said in a low voice. "Pack clothes for the journey. Warm clothes, for it will be cold in Maris. Then go to the bukshah fields and make Star ready. She will have to come with us to carry our supplies."

She waited for him to go, to do as she had asked, but he hesitated.

"Make haste now," she said sharply. "We leave at sunset."

Rowan stood where he was. "Please, Mother," he said. "Why do we have to go? How can you be this—this Chooser?"

"Jiller—you must tell him," Strong Jonn urged her. "You can delay no longer."

Jiller sighed. She closed the gate and gazed out over the crops that rippled like a green sea before her. "I am the Chooser because I was born to the task, Rowan," she said finally. "It is a duty that has been handed down through our family for hundreds of years."

"*Our* family?" Rowan could hardly believe what he was hearing. "But—why? And why did I not know of it before? Lann knew it. Jonn knew it. Timon knew it. Many must have known of it." He felt a quick rush of baffled anger. "Why did no one *tell* me?" he demanded.

"It is a thing known to few in Rin, by the wish of the Maris," said Jonn, putting a steadying hand on Rowan's shoulder.

"Perhaps I should have told you before now. But I did not want to trouble you until it was necessary," Jiller said, still looking straight ahead. "You have always been—one who worries about things, Rowan."

Rowan flinched. He knew very well that had he been a stronger, braver person, his mother would have shared the secret with him long ago.

She seemed to understand what he was feeling, for she glanced at him quickly, and touched his hand. "I wanted to protect you for as long as I could," she whispered. "That is all."

"Well, the time to tell the truth has come," said Strong Jonn. "Now Rowan must hear the whole story."

3 – The Chooser

nd so at last, pacing beneath the trees in the garden, Rowan heard the secret that his mother had kept from him for so long.

When the Zebak had invaded the coast, on the day Timon had called the most important in Rin's history, they had timed their arrival carefully. Their spies had told them that the Crystal of Maris was fading. The Keeper was dying. The Choosing of a new Keeper was about to begin.

The Zebak were sure that this was the perfect time to attack. Not only because the jealous Maris clans were busy plotting so that one of their own would be chosen as the new Keeper. But also because the Crystal itself was weak, and would not grow strong again until the Choosing was over.

The Zebak knew that the Choosing was governed by special rules, set down by Orin the Wise. Orin had real-ised that when he died, each clan would demand that one of its own must be Keeper. He did not want the power of the Crystal to be lost while the clans fought over it.

Orin's rules were simple. The Candidates for Keeper would go together to the Island in the Maris harbour. Not to fight, because the Maris did not greatly prize physical strength, but to take special tests of cleverness and cunning. The Candidates would be judged by a single Chooser. Whichever Candidate was chosen at the end of the tests would be the new Keeper of the Crystal.

Orin was clever, and he understood his people well. He knew that the Chooser had to be someone everyone could trust. So he decreed that the Chooser would always come from his own clan, the clan of Mirril. But in return for this honour no Mirril could ever again be Keeper of the Crystal.

The Mirril Chooser would select from only three Candidates—one from Fisk, one from Umbray, one from Pandellis. In this way the Chooser's clan would have nothing to lose or gain. The choice would always be fair.

The people accepted Orin's decree. It held for centuries—until something happened which even Orin himself could not have foreseen.

The Zebak attacked, while the old Keeper lay dying. And their very first act was to destroy the Mirril.

Not by chance. Not because the Mirril house was closest to the shore. But because they wanted to destroy the Chooser clan. They wanted to stop a new Keeper from being chosen. Then the Crystal would fade for ever, and victory would be theirs.

Their plan nearly succeeded. There were Candidates for Keeper, but with the Mirril all dead, there was no Chooser. And even in this crisis, with a battle raging on Maris shores, the Fisk, Pandellis and Umbray clans would not agree to leave the choice to one of their own. Nor would they leave it to the Keeper himself, who was in any case dying, and unable to move from the Cavern of the Crystal where he lay.

But the Zebak had forgotten one thing: the Crystal,

even dim, carried within it the wisdom of the ages. And the old Keeper, even dying, had the cunning of Orin himself.

The old Keeper knew where he could find a Chooser his people would accept. He turned to the strangers—the warrior slaves who had risen up against their Zebak masters and were fighting beside his own people. With the help of the Crystal, he selected a man to be the Chooser. That man was Jiller's ancestor, and Rowan's. His name was Lieth.

"So while the battle raged, Lieth went to the Island and chose the new Keeper," Jiller said. "The Crystal began to shine with new, radiant life. My father told me that its power is at its strongest when a new Keeper is chosen. And so it proved that day.

"Immediately, the tide of the battle turned. The Zebak were beaten and driven away. This land was saved. And our ancestors were freed from slavery, to start a new life."

"That was hundreds of years ago," said Rowan.

Jiller nodded. "It was. But the duty Lieth accepted at Maris that day has been passed down through our family ever since."

"It is a great honour," said Jonn quietly.

"A great honour, and at the same time, a curse." Jiller's face was set and pale.

"Why?" begged Rowan. "Why a curse?"

Jiller put out her hand, and grasped the latch of the door.

"Because to be a Chooser in Maris is to be in terrible danger," she whispered. "It is to risk death."

Suddenly she spun around, and took Rowan's face in

her hands. "I would give anything to spare you, Rowan. Anything. And yet I cannot spare you. I must take you with me, to take my place as Chooser should I die. And each of us must face whatever comes with courage. Each of us. Alone."

She dropped her hands from Rowan's cheeks, turned, and hurried into the house.

Rowan followed her inside. His mind was filled with confusion and fear. "Why, Mother? Why should we be in danger?" he cried. "Because of the Zebak? Because they know the time to attack the coast is when the Crystal is dim?"

"No!" Jiller cried sharply. Her eyes were fierce.

Rowan shrank back. It frightened him to see his mother like this. She was usually so calm and unafraid.

"Jiller!" Strong Jonn stepped forward. "Let us sit down. We will sit, eat and drink. And you can answer Rowan's questions as they should be answered. In peace."

"There is no time—" began Jiller, wringing her hands. And then, quite suddenly, she gave in. Her shoulders slumped. She pulled out a chair and sat down at the table.

"You are right," she said softly. "I am at fault. I have carried this burden alone for so long that it is hard for me to share it, now that the moment has come." She shook her head. "My father said the same thing to me, in his time."

"Did Grandfather choose a Keeper?" asked Rowan, sitting down timidly beside her. His grandfather had died when he was a small child. Rowan mainly remembered a wide, gentle smile, blue eyes, and hands, hard and rough from work in the fields, carving animals from wood with a small, sharp knife.

Jiller shook her head. "No, my father was never summoned," she said. "The present Keeper was chosen by his mother, my grandmother. But Father knew the Crystal would almost certainly dim in my lifetime. And it grieved him, very much."

Jonn put bread, cheese and milk on the table. "Eat, Jiller," he said. "And Rowan, you eat, too. You will need all your strength in the days to come. Missing meals will help nothing."

They began to eat the food. And Jonn was right, Rowan thought. Eating did help. He had not realised he was so hungry.

"So to be the Chooser is dangerous," he said, as calmly as he could. "Why is that?"

"It is because the Maris have not changed," growled Jonn. "The jealousy between the clans is like a madness." He put his hand on Jiller's arm. "Tell him the rest, Jiller."

Rowan's mother nodded reluctantly, and began to speak again.

"As each Keeper grows old, the Maris clans prepare for the Choosing. Each clan has at least one Candidate, trained from his or her earliest years for the tests to come. The people of each clan will do anything, anything at all, to make sure their Candidate will win. They will steal, spy, cheat and lie. They will even kill, if they suspect that the Chooser is favouring another."

She crumbled the bread on her plate, staring at it with unseeing eyes. "Many in our family have died in Maris. My great-grandfather was the last. Grieving and in fear, my grandmother, his first-born child, had to take his place as Chooser while he lay dead in the Cavern of the Crystal.

She did it bravely, it is said, though she was only fifteen."

Rowan felt his stomach turn over. But he forced himself to keep silent.

Jiller went on. "She had always known the danger. Many others in our family had died in the centuries before that, killed by jealous Candidates, or clan spies. Very, very often, the Choosing has brought death to the Chooser. Poison. Sharp blades in the dead of night. Bodies bound with nets and thrown into the hungry sea."

Rowan looked at his mother in horror. "But—that is madness."

Jonn nodded. "As I told you. Madness," he echoed. "A madness that has been going on for a thousand years."

"It is the Maris way," sighed Jiller. "There is no point in raging against it. Now, at least, the clans savage one another only when the Crystal dims. Once a new Keeper has been chosen, the Maris will come together again, swearing loyalty, and obeying their leader without question. So it has always been."

So it has always been ...

Rowan took a deep breath. "If both of us are killed," he said, in a level voice, "does that mean that Annad—?"

"No." Jiller smiled tiredly. "My one happiness is that Annad is too young to be summoned. If you and I should die, Rowan, the duty passes to another. To Timon. For his family is the next in line."

Timon. So that was why Timon's eyes had been so grave as he spoke of the Crystal of Maris.

Jonn pushed his plate away and stood up. "Well," he said, "we have talked, we have eaten, and now we must work. If we are to leave at sunset there is much to do."

Jiller looked up, startled. "*We?*" she asked. "You are not coming with us, are you, Jonn?"

"Of course," he said. "Do you think I would let you and Rowan go alone?"

She shook her head. "Jonn, this is my duty, and Rowan's. But there is no need for you to put yourself into danger also. No need."

"There is every need," Jonn said gently. "You know it. You know, too, that if Rowan's father were alive he would have gone with you to the coast. To be with Rowan while you are at the Choosing, if for nothing else. You must allow me the same right."

"We are betrothed, not married yet. And now, perhaps ..." Jiller's voice trembled, and she turned her face away.

Rowan felt his breath catch in his throat.

Jonn gripped the edge of the table, his eyes hard. "Do not say such things," he said loudly. "All will be well. You will be safe, and so will Rowan. I will see to it."

The words were brave. But Rowan knew that Jonn, for all his strength, could not protect them against what they were about to face. No one could protect them.

His mother's voice echoed in his mind.

Each of us must face whatever comes with courage. Each of us. Alone.

19

4 – The Journey

hey left at sunset. Few saw them go. Only Timon and old Lann came to the edge of the village to say farewell.

Annad was to stay with Marlie the weaver while Jiller and Rowan were away. She would be safe there, and happy. And she would feel important, too, for she was to care for the bukshah in Rowan's place.

"And if—" Jiller had whispered to Marlie. "If Rowan and I do not return ..."

"I will care for Annad as if she were my own," Marlie said quickly. "Do not fear. But, Jiller—you will return. You will."

Old Lann echoed those words, as she farewelled them.

"You will return," she said, her strong, wrinkled face showing none of the fear that perhaps she felt. "One of you at least will return. The summons has come late. The Maris man has told me that the Keeper is weakening very quickly. There will be no time to send to Rin for another Chooser. For which Timon, no doubt, is grateful."

Timon bowed his head. "That is not so. I would take Jiller's place willingly, if I could. But the Maris folk will not accept me as Chooser while she and Rowan live."

Lann glanced at Perlain, who was waiting impatiently

by the stream. "Maris is not what it was," she mumbled. "Bound hand and foot by rules, and following old ways, the people learn nothing. The Keepers guard the Crystal, but do not use it as once they did. They fear new ideas. They will not change. They will not grow. Yet the Zebak become more cunning with every year."

She frowned fiercely. "I beg you, Jiller, and you, Rowan of the Bukshah, if the duty comes to you, to choose wisely and well."

"I will try," Jiller murmured. Rowan swallowed, and nodded.

Lann bent forward. "And take care," she added in a harsh whisper. "Those slippery Maris devils will be watching you every moment. Now go. Our thoughts and our trust go with you."

* * *

For years, like every other child in Rin, Rowan had wanted to visit the coast. He had longed to gaze at the great ocean, sparkling, moving, blue as far as the eye could see.

He had imagined himself watching the mysterious, pale-skinned Maris folk sailing their boats into the sunrise, gliding like fish through the waves in the midday heat, mending nets at dusk. Safe at home in his green valley, he had shivered with pleasant fear at the thought of the huge, glistening coils and dripping jaws of the sea serpents, hunting their prey under the moon.

Rowan had seen so many pictures and heard so many stories about this place. He longed to see it all for himself.

He had thought he would travel to the home of the Maris on one of the Rin trading trips. Every year a group of villagers set out, excited and full of talk. Four or five

ts from the bukshah herd went with them,
gons loaded with cheese, fruit, vegetables,
hah wool and other goods.

Rowan always ran from his work in the bukshah fields
to watch them go. And three or four weeks later he stood
with the crowd to welcome them home again.

If trade had gone well, the Rin goods would be gone
from the wagons. In their place would be bundles of dried
fish, jars of oil, packages of salt and sponges.

The returning villagers would show the small things
they had bought for themselves and their friends: strange,
beautiful ornaments carved from driftwood and pearlshell, tiny, hard, speckled biscuits that tasted of the sea,
glittering fish-skin belts, necklaces bright with tiny
crystals. Rowan listened to their tales with excitement
and envy.

One day, he told himself, I will be old enough and
strong enough to go to the coast. One day ...

But that day had arrived far sooner than he had
expected. And it had come in a way that had shocked
him. For a reason he had never dreamed of.

* * *

The days and nights passed. It was a long journey. A hard
journey, too, for they travelled by night, and in haste.
Stumbling along the rough ground in the dark, following
first the stream and then the river that led to the sea, all of
them had grown very weary. Although they took what
rest they could during the day, it was difficult to sleep
deeply and long with the sun bright in the sky.

They travelled by night for the sake of Perlain, the
Maris man. Away from the sea spray his soft skin dried

and cracked. The sun of the inland, even at this gentle season, burned him.

He did not thank them for their care. He told them not to spare him. He said that time was too precious to waste. But after three nights of walking, he was too tired to argue further. He simply retreated into silence.

At night he flitted ahead of them, his feet soft on the grass, his blue clothes shining in the moonlight. During the day he soaked in the river while they slept on the bank.

One afternoon, when they were nearly at their journey's end, Rowan woke from an uneasy doze to see Perlain step dripping from the water, and sit down on the grass.

The shadows were long. Rowan knew that soon it would be time for them to eat and be on their way once more. But Jiller and Jonn were still asleep. Even Star was dozing. On an impulse, Rowan got up and went over to the Maris man.

Perlain watched him approach. His flat eyes showed neither surprise nor welcome.

Rowan had thought he might try to talk to Perlain, ask him questions about Maris. But now he found he did not know how to begin. He stared at him dumbly, very aware of the Maris man's odd appearance, his strange, fishy smell.

"Did you sleep well, First-born of the Chooser?" Perlain asked politely.

"Yes, thank you," lied Rowan. "Did you?"

Perlain shrugged, and his thin lips curved into a smile. "I will be home by morning," he said simply.

He looked at the sky. "It is time for the Chooser to awake," he said. Obviously he wanted Rowan to leave him.

Rowan bit his lip. "Perlain," he said, in a rush. "The Crystal of Maris. Could you tell me about it?"

Perlain stared. "I am only the Keeper's Messenger. I do not know all the secrets of the Crystal."

"I do not want to know the secrets," Rowan pleaded. "Just the things everyone in Maris must know. Even we in Rin know a little. The Crystal was found long ago by a man called Orin the Wise. I know that. But I do not know where it was found, or how. Could you not tell me that, at least?"

Perlain seemed to consider for a moment. Then, slowly, he nodded. "I will tell you what I know," he said.

He looked out across the river.

"Orin was fishing, unwisely, as the sun went down," he began. "The full moon had risen. The Great Serpent, the mother of all the other serpents of the sea, rose from the dark water, upset Orin's boat, and hunted him to the Island in the harbour."

Rowan shuddered. In the house of books there was a picture of the Great Serpent of Maris. It had always filled him with true fear. A huge, twisting, scaly beast, with the head of a dragon and the body of a giantic snake, rose from the sea. A boat filled with screaming Maris folk, their hands pressed to their ears, was crushed in its terrible, dripping jaws.

Perlain smiled slightly, and went on. "In his terror, Orin fled into a cave, and from there he plunged through a dark tunnel that led deep below the sea.

"In a small, rocky cavern, he found the Crystal. When he touched it, it began to glow—as though a hundred rainbow fires were trapped inside it. He stayed in the cavern all night, and the next morning he carried the Crystal to the shore.

"The people knew at once that the Crystal was a great wonder, though in those days no one realised just how powerful it was. They soon found that it shone only for Orin. And they saw that he had been changed by it. Suddenly he could see things they could not. Feel fish below the surface of the sea. Sense serpents lurking. Taste the wind and say when storms were coming. Even see into other people's hearts.

"And Orin was changed in other ways. Before he found the Crystal he had been filled with hatred for clans not his own. Yet now, though his clan urged him to use his new power to destroy its rivals, he would not. He shared with everyone the knowledge and wisdom of the Crystal."

"So he became the Maris leader," Rowan put in. "The first Keeper."

"Yes. By the power of the Crystal," said Perlain. "And then everything happened as he had said it would. Once the people put their minds to building, and planning, and gathering food, instead of warring with one another, our nation prospered. Other Keepers followed Orin, each chosen according to the rules he laid down. And the Crystal—"

"Yes," Rowan prompted him eagerly. "What of the Crystal?"

"As the years went on, it was found that the Crystal was more, much more, than even Orin had thought."

Perlain hesitated, then continued, choosing his words carefully. "The Crystal does not just give. It takes and keeps, also. It now contains all the knowledge of Maris. When an old Keeper dies, all his learning and experience passes into the Crystal. And from there it passes into the new Keeper. So nothing is lost. Everything is remembered."

"So each Keeper is wiser than the Keepers of the past!" breathed Rowan. "Wiser and more powerful."

"So it is said."

"No wonder, then, that to be Keeper is a great prize," said Rowan. "Everyone in Maris must long to be chosen as a Candidate."

"Oh, no," Perlain answered softly. "Not everyone. I for one cannot think of anything I would care for less."

And then, suddenly seeming to feel he had said too much, he jumped lightly to his feet and moved away.

Rowan looked out over the river. The water ran swiftly, carrying sticks and leaves with it, moving endlessly towards the ocean.

Tomorrow, Rowan thought, we will be where that water is going. We will be at the place where the river meets the sea.

Tomorrow, we will be in Maris.

5 – Danger

Footsore, cold, and tired to his bones, Rowan felt the stinging wind in his face, tasted salt on his lips, and stared with watering eyes at the endless, wave-capped sea. His hand reached for the comforting warmth of Star's rough mane.

Star rumbled deep in her throat and swayed against him. Like Rowan, she was far from home. She longed for the sweet air of the valley of Rin, and the soft grass of the bukshah fields.

She did not like the chill wind that blew the salt spray into her small black eyes and the sharp, fishy scent into her tender nose. She did not like the sand and pebbles under her hoofs. She did not like the dim stable where she was tethered, or the strange, silent people who stared at her as they passed.

"You will feel better when you have rested, Star," Rowan murmured to her, rubbing her nose. "We will all feel better then."

He knew he was talking to himself as much as to her.

The wind blew harder. Star pawed the ground, turning her head away from the stable door, away from the noise of the wind, and the stinging sand.

"I must go now," said Rowan. "Jonn will be waiting for me. But I will be back to see you soon."

Star rumbled unhappily.

"Your water is here, and your food. Eat and drink, now, then sleep," Rowan urged her. "Sleeping will make the time pass more quickly."

He patted Star's humped neck one more time, then turned away. He hoped his comforting words were true. He hated leaving Star alone, locked up like this. But the Maris had nowhere else to keep her.

At least here she will be safe, Rowan thought, as he barred the stable door behind him and began trudging along the pebbled street to the place where he and Jonn were to stay. The stable was strong, built of the rock-like bricks the Maris made and used for their own houses. The fearsome creatures that slithered from the sea to hunt in the darkness of the night could not break those strong walls down.

Perlain had told him this, smiling slightly, with his head on one side. It was not the way of the Maris people to bond closely with animals. Perlain was amused that Rowan cared so much for Star, but he was far too polite to say so.

Rowan looked out again into the harbour, where the Island hunched, dark and covered with thick forest, beaten by waves and wind. He could see no movement on its rocky shore, but his mother might already be there, hidden among the trees. She had been taken away as soon as they arrived in Maris. And that was a couple of hours ago at least.

Rowan and Jonn had been told that she would go first to the Cavern of the Crystal and then to the Island. There she would stay until the Choosing was complete.

Rowan gazed at the glittering sea and the black shape of the Island, but he did not really see them. He no longer saw the shore of Maris, or the hard, pebbled street on which he stood, or the rounded houses that crowded one against the other behind him. He no longer noticed the curious glances of the passing Maris folk.

In his mind, he was back in Rin, standing by the bukshah pool. The bukshah rumbled and snorted around him. His mother was working in the fields. Strong Jonn was in the orchard. All was quiet. All was safe ...

Rowan felt a hand on his shoulder, and jumped. He spun around to see Perlain looking at him enquiringly.

"What are you doing here, alone, First-born of the Chooser?" the Maris man asked. "Why are you not in the safe house, with Jonn of the Orchard, where I left you?"

"I—I was seeing to Star, my bukshah," stammered Rowan.

A weary smile crossed Perlain's face. "You people of Rin are very strange," he sighed. "Do you want to be found tomorrow morning in a ditch, stabbed to the heart, my friend? Is this beast, this bukshah, so important that you would risk that?"

"There is no reason why anyone should wish to kill me, Perlain," said Rowan stoutly. "I have done no harm to anyone. And I do not know anything about the Choosing, as yet. I have not even seen the Candidates. No one could know how I would vote, should it be left to me."

A cloud seemed to veil Perlain's pale eyes for a moment, then once more his mouth curved in a smile. "You are wiser than you seem, Rowan of Rin," he murmured. "And

29

yet not as wise as you believe. The Candidates study the ways of Rin, and your family more than any. Their trainers know how you think. They have collected news of you since the day you were born."

Rowan's cheeks grew hot, despite the icy wind. He did not like to think of his life being spied on from a distance by cold, pale-eyed strangers. He glanced at Perlain, and his face showed clearly how he felt.

The Maris man spread his small webbed hands.

"That is how it has always been," he said. "It is best that you understand. Come with me now, to the safe house. And I would suggest that from now on you wait there, and that you do not go into the streets alone."

He took Rowan by the arm and drew him on down the pebbled street.

"I have to visit Star at least twice a day," said Rowan stubbornly. "To fill her water bowl, and give her food. She is lonely, and perhaps afraid."

"And you are not afraid?" Perlain stared at him. His flat eyes seemed to pierce Rowan's soul. Then he nodded. "Oh, yes. I see it now. You are afraid, but you are trying not to show that you are. This is the way of Rin, is it not?"

Rowan said nothing. He walked on, feeling Perlain's cool breath on his cheek. He saw the other Maris people, especially those who wore the silver and green of the Umbray and Fisk clans, staring and whispering as they passed. Perhaps they were wondering what Perlain was saying to him. Wondering if Perlain was taking advantage of his place as the Keeper's Messenger. If he was singing the praises of the Candidate from the clan of Pandellis. Just in case the First-born should become the Chooser.

The low voice went on, close to his ear. "Yet you are different from others I have met. Different from the loud, large people who come to trade with us each year. Different from your tall, brave mother, the Chooser. Your eyes have the look of one who has seen the Great Serpent, and lived. Deep, and full of knowledge. Strange in a boy so young. I have known only one other."

Rowan stumbled, and looked down at his feet, not knowing what to say.

"You keep silence," said Perlain. "This is good. In silence, you are safe." He stopped, and pointed. "There is your safe house," he said. "I will go with you no further. Food will be brought to you soon. Our finest fish. The eggs of the Kirrian Worm, gathered fresh from the sands this morning. But I suggest you keep to your own supplies."

"Why?" asked Rowan.

Perlain shrugged. "You may find that something in a Maris dish does not agree with you," he said calmly. "Tell your friend Jonn, if you wish. If you value his life as much as you value your own."

He bowed and moved away, slipping like a blue shadow down a narrow lane between two houses and disappearing from sight.

Rowan paced the last few steps to the small building where he was to stay with Jonn.

Perlain was warning him of poison. Poisoned food, poisoned drink.

Jiller had taken her own food and drink with her to the Island. She, Rowan and Jonn had all agreed on this. But they had not thought that Jonn and Rowan would have to take similar care. Not so soon. Not unless the worst happened, and Jiller was killed.

The people of each clan will do anything, anything at all, to make sure their Candidate will win. They will steal, spy, cheat and lie. They will even kill, if they suspect that the Chooser is favouring another.

Take care, Mother, thought Rowan, pressing his hands together. Do not let anyone know how you are feeling. Do not even hint at which Candidate you think the best. Guard your words, and your face, and even your thoughts …

For perhaps, after a thousand years of the Crystal, the Keeper was not the only one in Maris who could read thoughts. Rowan remembered how Perlain's pale eyes had searched his. Perlain had seemed to know what he was thinking. Could it be? If so, then Jiller could not be safe, however careful she was.

She would not be safe until she was back in the Cavern of the Crystal, until she had put a hand on the shoulder of one of the Candidates and had said the words she had whispered to Rowan on the journey to this place. The words every Chooser had said since the time of Orin.

The Chooser has made the Choice. Let the other Candidates leave this place.

Rowan found that he was panting with fear. Deliberately, he slowed his breath. He rubbed his sweating hands on his shirt. He knew he had to keep calm. As calm as his mother would want him to be. But it was hard. So hard.

He wondered for the thousandth time whether Jiller had been right to keep their family's secret from him all these years. Would it have been better to have been prepared?

32

Or would the story have burdened his childhood, as it was burdening him now? Would he have worried about it, and feared every day the coming of the Maris messenger? Would his dreams have been haunted by pale, watchful people with cold eyes and webbed hands, a rocky black island circled by foam, a crystal burning like fire?

Rowan heard a sound and looked up. The people on the street were parting to let a hurrying group through. A group of three, two men and a woman, wearing capes that flapped and snapped in the wind.

One man wore the silver of Umbray, the other the blue of Pandellis. The woman wore the green of Fisk. Their faces were serious. They were coming straight towards him. Something had happened. Something terrible.

Rowan's whole body began to shake. His heart felt as though it was bursting. He heard muttering around him as a crowd gathered to watch. The three Maris stopped in front of him, and bowed low. The man in blue glanced at the others and began to speak.

"Chooser of Rin, who holds the fate of Maris in your hands, I greet you in the name of the Keeper of the Crystal ..." he began.

As his voice droned on, whispers rose from the crowd on the street, filling Rowan's ears, rising and falling, hissing like wave-foam on the sand. Chooser ... Chooser ... the mother ... Poison ... Poison ... Poison ...

And as the red tide of horror rose and flooded Rowan's mind, a single thought floated to the surface. Jiller had been right to keep him in ignorance for as long as she could. For nothing she could have told him would have prepared him for this agony. Nothing at all.

6 – Poison

Who has done this?" Rowan heard his own voice speaking as though from far away.

"There is no way of telling," said the taller of the men, the man of Umbray. "Your mother fell ill on the Island. She was there alone with the Candidates. The Choosing had just begun." His face showed no expression at all. His flat eyes were cold.

One of the Candidates, thought Rowan. Someone who thought they were going to lose. His head swam.

There is no way of telling.

But there had to be.

The green-clad woman looked at the sun. "We must hurry," she said. "The Crystal dims. The Choosing must go on. Time flows away from us like the tide." She began to move away.

Blindly, Rowan caught at her arm to hold her back. His fingers slipped on the smooth surface of the garment she wore. Beneath the fabric the flesh felt cool and slightly damp.

"Jonn! Does Jonn know?" he burst out, glancing at the closed door of the safe house just ahead.

"Not yet," she said.

"He must be told!"

"He will be. And would know already, had you been with him as expected," she said. "We were surprised to see you on the street alone." Her voice was icy: her disapproval was very clear.

"I wasn't—" Rowan broke off, biting back the words. He had been going to say that he hadn't been alone. That Perlain had been with him. But with a stab of fear that had pierced even the pain and confusion he was feeling, he realised that to admit this would be dangerous now.

Perlain was of the Pandellis clan. If the Fisk and Umbray people thought the Chooser was becoming too friendly with a Pandellis man, even the Keeper's Messenger, they might be jealous. They might decide that Rowan would be sure to choose the Pandellis Candidate for Keeper. They might—

"Come," said a quiet voice beside him. It was the Umbray man. His face was so close that Rowan could see his own reflection in the colourless eyes.

"Come," the man repeated. "We must delay no longer. You are the Chooser now. The fate of Maris is in your hands."

"I want to see my mother," Rowan managed to say.

The man nodded. "Of course. That is why she has been carried to the Cavern of the Crystal, by order of the Keeper. You must bid her farewell before you take her place on the Island, Chooser of Rin. She will no longer be alive by the time you return."

Rowan's heart gave an enormous leap. "You mean she still—*lives?*" he gasped. "I thought ..."

"She breathes," murmured the Umbray man, turning

his face towards the crashing sea. "But her heart beats ever more slowly as the poison spreads within her. Soon she will breathe no more."

"She does not suffer," the Pandellis man added quickly, glancing at Rowan's stricken face. "She sleeps, and dreams, and with every dream she slips further away from the shore of life. That is all."

The Umbray man smiled, thin-lipped. "Do not pretend to the Chooser that you are soft-hearted like him and his people, Pandellis. The whole of Maris knows that the Pandellis are born with chips of ice floating in their veins. That they are cold and feel nothing. Whereas the Umbray—"

The Fisk woman whirled around to face him. "The Umbray are as bad as the Pandellis. They are simply better at deceiving, slippery as the eels that coil in the river slime," she spat. "My clan, however—"

"Shut your serpent's mouth, Fisk!" growled the Umbray man, raising a shimmering silver arm.

The three stepped closer to one another, crowding Rowan between them. Their voices rose, loud and bitter. Around them the crowd muttered, drawing into separate groups. Pandellis. Umbray. Fisk. Webbed hands felt for knives, long and narrow. Blades flashed and glittered in the sun.

Rowan's head was spinning. He looked around at the strange pale faces, twisted with fury, the thin wide lips, open, shouting, the flat eyes glazed with anger.

Hot rage rose within him. He hated these people. He hated them all. Their stupid, murderous rivalry had killed his mother.

He gritted his teeth. "Stop it!" he shouted, clapping his hands to his ears. "*Stop it!*"

With quick, hissing breaths, the Maris stiffened, fell silent and drew back. Their faces grew watchful.

The wind wailed, the waves crashed on the shore.

A lump rose in Rowan's throat. He felt as though he was choking. His eyes burned with tears. He swallowed and blinked to hold them back.

At last he found his voice.

"Take me to the Cavern of the Crystal," he said. "Take me to my mother! Now!"

* * *

As Rowan walked, he stared straight ahead at the slim back of the Umbray man who led the way. Dimly he was aware of the Fisk woman gliding along on his left, the Pandellis man on his right. They weren't very much taller than he was, yet now that his sudden rage had died, leaving numbness behind, he felt trapped by them. Hemmed in, surrounded, helpless.

Swiftly the group moved through the streets, cutting through the green, blue and silver of the milling crowd like a great fish through water.

"The Chooser ... the Chooser ..." Rowan heard the voices as he passed. The people were talking about him. They knew. They knew what had happened to his mother. Perhaps some of them even knew who had poisoned her, and why.

Soon she will breathe no more.

The words were so final. And yet ... Rowan quickened his pace until he was almost treading on the Umbray man's heels. How did the Maris know this for sure? They did not know his mother. They did not know her strength. Perhaps even now something could be done to help her.

"How much further?" he demanded aloud. Suddenly he was terrified that Jiller would die before he reached her.

"No further," said the Pandellis man briefly. "We have arrived." His shoulder touched Rowan's as they made a sharp turn to the right, towards the sea.

Waves crashed and pounded. Rowan felt spray on his face. He looked up and around.

They were standing in front of a rounded, sand-coloured building with huge doors covered in gleaming pearlshell. On the roof was a cupped shape where a flame would burn to tell the whole of Maris that the Choosing was completed and that the Chooser was about to name the new Keeper. Now it was cold and empty.

In front of the building was a courtyard of pale green stones. Behind it was the sea, dashing itself against the rocks. And across the water, ringed with white foam, was the darkness of the Island.

The Umbray man stopped, and stood aside. "You must enter alone, Chooser of Rin," he said with careful respect.

The woman of Fisk made a quick movement, as though she was about to speak. But then she appeared to change her mind. She looked down at her hands, and kept silence.

Rowan felt, rather than saw, the three Maris people watching him as he walked towards the building. He no longer cared what they did, or what they thought. As he pushed open the shining doors and entered the strange round room beyond, he did not even feel afraid. It was as though he was beyond feeling anything. As though he was watching himself in a dream.

The doors swung closed behind him and he found that he was alone.

The room was large. Its walls and ceiling were curved. They, and the floor, were made of polished stone, hard, smooth and shining. Candles burning in holders fixed to the floor gave the only light.

A stairway in one corner led downwards.

Rowan went to the head of the stairway. Below, he could see light glimmering. He put his hand on the railing, and his foot on the first stair.

Welcome, Chooser of Rin.

The voice echoed in Rowan's brain. His head jerked up. Shocked, he looked around.

I am below. Come to me.

The voice was soft, beckoning. Rowan obeyed it.

He knew that he was about to meet the Keeper of the Crystal.

7 – The Keeper

he stairs wound down, down. Rowan lost count of them. He realised that he was under the earth, under the sea. A soft, blue-green glow lit his way. The walls on either side of him were stone, and the steps themselves were stone, hard and cold under his feet. There was the sound of dripping water and the smell of salt and sea plants.

With every step he took, the more his feeling grew that something was drawing him in. His legs seemed to be moving without his willing it. It was as though he was being pulled down through water by an invisible net.

Fear rose in him, overwhelming every other feeling, every thought.

He shivered, and gripped the railing till his knuckles turned white. He wanted to sink down to the cold stone. He wanted to claw his way back up to the surface. But still he moved down, down.

Do not be afraid. It is the Crystal's power you feel. It will not harm you. And your mother is here with me.

The voice filled his mind, lapping over his fear, washing it away, leaving sorrow and shame in its place.

Mother, Rowan thought. Mother is there. How could

I have forgotten? How could I have hesitated? Even for a minute?

Now his fear seemed like madness. Holding tightly to the railing to stop himself from stumbling, he moved on. The blue-green light grew brighter. The sound of dripping water grew louder.

At last he saw that he was nearly at the bottom of the stairs. Ahead, there was a wall of shining rock. And cut into it was an archway, curtained by falling drops of water that glittered like tiny crystals in the light that flooded from the Cavern beyond.

We are here.

Rowan no longer needed the voice to lead him. He could feel the power of the Crystal, beaming out from the Cavern as strongly as the light.

He stepped from the last stair and in two strides had plunged through the watery veil. Chill, salty droplets pattered softly on his face, filled his eyes and clung to his hair. Then he felt sand beneath his feet. He looked up. Through a blur he saw gleaming rock walls, running with water, and light.

"Again, welcome, Chooser of Rin."

This time the voice had spoken aloud. Whispering, husky, ancient, it echoed from the dripping walls over and over again till every corner of the Cavern seemed filled with the sound. There was no way of telling where the speaker was. Rowan rubbed at his eyes, looked wildly around.

Blue-green light flooded the space, so that the air was like deep, clear water lit by the sun. The source of the light was somewhere in the centre of the room, but Rowan did

41

not even glance at it. For to one side, on a couch draped with silken cloth, was Jiller.

He ran to her, dropping onto his knees beside the couch. She was very still. Her eyes were closed. The hand he touched was cool. But when he put his face close to hers he could feel her soft breath. It was as though she was simply asleep.

She sleeps. She dreams. And with every dream she slips further away from the shore of life.

"Mother," he whispered. "Mother, it's me. It's Rowan." Drops of water from his face and hair fell on her cheek. He brushed them away.

The pale lips slowly curved into a faint smile. Rowan's heart thumped. She could hear him! He gripped her hand tightly.

"Mother, wake up," he begged. "You must fight the dreams. Fight the poison. You are strong. You must not die! You must live! For Annad. For Jonn. For me!"

A tiny line appeared between Jiller's eyebrows, and her eyelids flickered.

"Do not disturb her peace, Rowan," whispered a voice. "She cannot wake. Say farewell, and let her rest. You are the Chooser now."

Rowan spun around. But the words of anger he had been about to utter died on his lips when he met the eyes of the being who had spoken.

The Keeper of the Crystal was sitting motionless in the centre of the room, bathed in light.

She did not look old as the people of Rin looked old. She was not wrinkled like Lann. But Rowan knew at once that never had he seen a living creature so ancient. She seemed almost transparent. She was so faded, so thin and shrunken, and her delicate skin was so fine and pale, that it was difficult to see her clearly against the background of her chair.

And her eyes! They were huge in her tiny face. They seemed to speak of the wisdom and the knowledge of ages, and, above all, of a terrible yearning for rest. Such things I have seen, the eyes seemed to say. Such things I have known. But now I am tired. So tired.

Her tiny hands, the webs between the fingers almost transparent, spread lovingly over the source of the light— a huge, glowing crystal she held on her lap. Now she bent slowly towards it. The light flooded her face, and she shut her eyes, as if basking in warmth.

"The Candidates are waiting for you, Rowan of Rin," she said. "The Choosing must go on without delay. My time draws near."

Rowan felt himself begin to shiver all over. "One of the Candidates gave my mother poison," he said.

"It may be," answered the Keeper.

"Which one?"

"I cannot tell. The Crystal is dim. I no longer see as far as the Island. And I cannot read the thoughts of those trained to veil their minds, as the Candidates have been from earliest childhood. The poison is an ancient Mirril brew called Death Sleep. It has not been seen in Maris for centuries. It kills slowly, but surely. That is all I can tell you."

The Mirril. Experts in poison. Suddenly Rowan was back in Rin, under the Teaching Tree, listening to Timon's tales of the clans of Maris. The Mirril. Experts in poison. And for every poison …

The whispering voice went on, breaking into his memories. "Rowan! Attend to me! Time is short. You must continue the Choosing."

"How can I continue?" Rowan demanded. "How can I, knowing that one of the Candidates is a murderer? While my mother lies here, slipping away from life?"

"You can because you must. As your ancestors have done before you," said the Keeper. "And the Mirril Choosers before them. So it has always been." She hunched over the Crystal. Waiting.

"Just because a thing has always been, that does not mean it must always be." The words burst from Rowan before he thought about them.

The Keeper breathed a long sigh. Slowly she opened her eyes.

Rowan glanced behind him, at his mother lying on the couch. He knew what she would say to this. She would urge him to be strong. To accept the pain, and do his duty. As her grandmother did. As she would have done. As the people of their family had done for centuries.

"Yes," said the Keeper, as he turned back to face her. "You must be strong."

She had read his mind.

Rowan looked straight into her face. "I will be strong, Keeper of Maris," he said. "I will be strong in my own way."

In the Keeper's eyes he thought he saw a spark, like an ember flaring suddenly in a dying fire. Perhaps it was anger. Perhaps it was surprise. Or—something else. It was impossible to tell. No movement disturbed the smoothness of her face.

"There must be an antidote for Death Sleep," Rowan said.

She shook her head. "Nothing can be done." She bent her head to the Crystal once more.

Rowan clenched his fists. She was lying to him. He knew it. Again he remembered Timon's words.

The Mirril. Experts in poison. A thousand and one deadly poisons. And for every poison, an antidote.

For every problem, a solution. For every poison, an antidote.

But there was no way that he could make the Keeper tell what she must know. Her mind was fixed on the Choosing. On the need for haste. She was not willing to spend precious time searching for a cure for Jiller. Old and wise and rich in knowledge she might be, but she was still a Maris.

"The death of one is of no account," Perlain had gasped in the Rin village square.

That was the Maris way.

But old Lann had answered, "This is your belief, but not ours."

"Not ours," Rowan said under his breath.

The Crystal glowed. Somewhere beyond the Cavern he heard a grating sound, as of a door sliding open.

"I have summoned the Candidates," said the Keeper. She raised herself from the Crystal and leaned back in her chair.

Again the Crystal glowed. Still the Keeper's face did not change. Yet Rowan had the feeling that her mind was fixed on something outside the room.

"Your friend Jonn of the Orchard approaches," she said.

"But I must deny him entry to the Cavern. Jonn is full of sorrow and anger. He wishes to avenge your mother's death."

"My mother is not dead," said Rowan loudly. His voice echoed. *Not dead. Not dead.*

On the silk-covered couch, Jiller stirred.

There was a sound from the back of the room.

"Enter," said the Keeper.

Three figures stood framed in the doorway. One wore silver, one blue, one green.

Rowan stared at them. He had expected the Candidates to be at least as old as his mother, or Jonn. But these people were much younger. For a moment this surprised him. Then he remembered that the Crystal brought with it the knowledge and memories of a thousand years of Maris history. Age and experience of life were not important qualities for the Candidates: just the tests of brainpower, set down by Orin the Wise, for which they had studied all their lives. Intelligence was important. Determination was important.

And a will to win is important, thought Rowan savagely. And, it seems, a murderous heart. He went on watching the figures by the door. His mind was cold with loathing.

One of you had a reason to cheat my mother of life, he thought. And you think you have succeeded. But somehow I am going to defeat you. And no one, not even the Keeper of the Crystal, is going to stop me.

8 – The Candidates

Asha of Umbray," said the Keeper.

The silver-clad figure stepped forward and bowed. She was tall, for a Maris, and looked down at Rowan, meeting his gaze without flinching.

"I greet you, Chooser of Rin," she said in a level voice. "The fate of Maris is in your hands."

Are you the one? Rowan thought, staring deep into her steady, pale grey eyes. Could you look at me like this if you had poisoned my mother, Asha? Perhaps you could, for the Umbray are skilled at deceiving, I am told. Slippery, like the eels that coil in the river slime. Did you find my strong, practical mother difficult to twine around your finger? Did you think it would be easier to impress a younger, more timid Chooser? A boy? Like me?

"Seaborn of Fisk," droned the Keeper's voice.

The green figure bowed and repeated Asha's words. He was even taller than she was, and looked stronger. He stood straight, and held his arms rigidly by his sides. But he spoke softly, and as he spoke his eyes kept drifting to the still figure on the couch, and back to the Keeper's chair.

Or is it you who is guilty, Seaborn of Fisk? thought Rowan. Is that why you cannot look at me? Was it you who slipped the poison into the Chooser's food or drink, thinking that as a woman she might favour the girl Asha instead of you? Or do your eyes slide away from mine because you are disappointed, brave, strong Fisk? Did you think my mother was going to choose you? Are you sorry that now you must face me in her place?

"Doss of Pandellis," said the Keeper.

The blue figure stepped forward, and again the bow, and the words, were repeated.

Doss was younger than the other Candidates. He was slighter and smaller, too, and his eyes seemed darker, deeper and more mysterious.

A memory floated into Rowan's mind. Perlain, looking at him curiously. Perlain's words: *Your eyes have the look of one who has seen the Great Serpent, and lived. Deep, and full of knowledge. Strange in a boy so young. I have known only one other.*

Are you Perlain's "other", Doss? thought Rowan. You are of the Pandellis clan, like him. Did Perlain see in me something that reminded him of you? Did others see it? Others in your clan? Did they tell you? Did they think that I would feel closer to you than my mother would? That I would be more likely to choose you? Is that why ...?

"The Chooser is ready, Candidates," said the Keeper. "He has only to join with the Crystal, in place of his mother. Then you can return to the Island, and the Choosing can once again begin."

The three bowed their heads.

Join with the Crystal? thought Rowan. What does that mean? Could this be my chance? He felt a small flutter of fearful hope.

"I tell you all," the Keeper warned. "If anything should happen to this boy, as happened to his mother, there will be no time to begin the Choosing for a third time."

She twisted her chair around to face them.

"The Crystal dims," she croaked, looking at them one by one. "Soon I shall die. And if no new Keeper stands beside me at my death, to take the Crystal's knowledge from me and renew its power, the Crystal too will die. Then the Maris clans will be divided once more, and with the Crystal dimmed for ever there will be no protection when the Zebak come again to our shores, as certainly they will. For us, and for this land, all will be lost."

Lost, lost, lost, whispered the echoes.

The Candidates lifted their heads and stood silent.

"Give me your hand, Chooser of Rin," said the Keeper.

Rowan hesitated. His heart was hammering in his chest. He forced himself to be calm. "Please explain to me why I must do this," he said quietly.

Again, something flickered in the Keeper's eyes. Anger? thought Rowan. Amusement?

"The Crystal must know you, through me," she said. "Once this has happened, it will recognise you as the only Chooser. Please hurry. Jonn of the Orchard is very near. I would have this finished before he arrives demanding entry."

Rowan stepped forward. With his whole being he concentrated, hiding his thoughts, waiting for the moment.

I will be strong in my own way.

He stretched out his hand. The Keeper's webbed fingers touched his. Soft, cool, damp. Rowan felt a tingling running up his arm.

Now, he thought. He shut his eyes and gripped the fingers tightly. Then he toppled, fell, plunged into the deep, deep water of the Keeper's mind, the Keeper's memories.

Pictures.

Beauty, and light. Waves curling, blue-green, breaking to hissing white foam on golden sand. A child, laughing, free, ducking, diving, playing, with friends. Long, long ago ...

Study, teachers, advisors, candles burning far into the night. The Crystal, bright as the sun, beckoning. A world shrunk to a cavern beneath the earth ...

Panicking, Rowan struggled, falling deeper. Into older minds, older memories.

Ancient seas. Creatures twisting, hunting, hidden under glittering water ... the Great Serpent towering above me, fangs dripping poison ...

Poison. Rowan caught the word, and held it like a lifeline. He shut out the swirling pictures. Made his own picture.

Jiller, my mother. Poisoned. Lying so still. Dreaming while her life slips away.

He fixed his mind on the picture, and the words Death Sleep. *Tell me*, he demanded. *Tell me, Keeper.*

The Crystal dims ... I am so tired ... there is no time ...

Tell me!

And then, suddenly, something gave way, and the answer was there before his eyes. He saw a jar, held in small webbed hands. The jar was half filled with silvery liquid. As Rowan watched, the liquid changed colour, becoming as blue as the sky. The blue changed to green. Then the liquid changed again, losing all colour, becoming crystal clear. And a voice spoke.

"To mix the brew that wakes Death Sleep
Fill one spread hand with silver deep.
In hungry pool moons raise their heads:
Pluck one and add the tears it sheds.
Stir slowly with new fighter's quill,
Three times, no more, and let it still.
Add venom from your greatest fear—
One drop—and then the truth is clear."

With a gasp of triumph, Rowan broke free. He staggered back from the Keeper's chair. His mind was spinning. His hand was burning.

Slowly he opened his eyes. He saw darkness, shot with darts and swirls of colour. Then, at last, his sight cleared.

The Keeper was slumped back in her chair. Her eyes were closed. The Crystal pulsed dimly under her limp hands. Behind the chair stood Asha, Seaborn and Doss, staring at him as though he were some demon from the deep.

"What have you done?" breathed Seaborn.

"What I had to do," said Rowan. The words sounded strong, but he was not feeling strong at all. His legs wobbled like the legs of a new-born bukshah calf. The hand with which he had gripped the Keeper's fingers still throbbed and burned.

The Keeper's eyelids fluttered and opened.

"Keeper—" Asha began. But the ancient woman did not even glance at her. Her whole attention was fixed on Rowan.

"What do you want?" she asked bluntly.

Rowan did not have the chance to answer, for at that moment there was the sound of thudding feet on stone steps, and Strong Jonn burst through the curtain of dripping water, into the Cavern.

He looked around rapidly, taking in everything in a single glance. Then he strode to Jiller's side and bent over her. He gathered her in his arms, lifting her to his chest, calling her name. She did not stir.

He turned to Rowan, grim-faced. "She spoke of danger, but I did not really believe," he said. "I thought, no, not Jiller. Nothing could happen to Jiller. Rowan——"

"It will be all right, Jonn," said Rowan quietly. "There is an antidote for the poison Mother has been given. The Keeper has just shown it to me."

There was a gasp from behind the Keeper's chair. Rowan looked up quickly. Asha? Seaborn? Doss? He could not tell.

"I will not let Mother die," he said. And he was telling himself, and everyone in the room, as well as Jonn.

"The Choosing must continue," said the Keeper urgently.

Rowan turned to face her.

"No," he said. He heard his own voice shaking as the word echoed around the Cavern walls. "I am sorry, but the Choosing must wait."

He felt Jonn's eyes fixed on him. He knew that Asha, Seaborn and Doss were staring, too. But he could see only the Keeper.

"I know that time is short," he said. "But before anything else can be done my mother must have the antidote to Death Sleep. You must give it to me, Keeper. Or tell me where to find it. I must help my mother. Nothing is more important than that."

9 – The Rhyme

You said you would be strong, Rowan of Rin," the Keeper accused him. "You let me join you to the Crystal, confirm you as Chooser. You deceived me."

"I said I would be strong in my own way," said Rowan, trying desperately to sound calm and firm while his legs trembled beneath him. "You must tell me what I must do to save my mother."

"It is impossible!" the Keeper said. She clawed at the Crystal with her tiny hands as though willing it to save her from what was happening. But it only glowed feebly.

"Speak to him!" she ordered the Candidates. But they stood silent, wondering.

The Keeper took a deep breath. "I told you. Death Sleep has not been used in Maris since the time of the Mirril."

Rowan glanced at Jonn. He had put Jiller down and was standing beside her couch, his fists clenched. Rowan knew what he was thinking. If the poison was so rare it should not be too difficult to find out where it had come from. To find out which clan had discovered the Mirril secret, and used it.

But Rowan was not interested in revenge. Not now.

"There is an antidote," he repeated. "I saw it, Keeper. A

silver liquid, changing to blue, then green, then becoming clear. I saw it, held in Maris hands."

The Keeper's steady gaze did not waver. "The hands were Orin's," she said.

"Orin," whispered Asha. Seaborn raised his hand to his mouth. Doss remained expressionless.

"Orin was making the antidote to Death Sleep on the Island, the day he found the Crystal," the Keeper said. "That is what you saw in my mind, Chooser of Rin. You saw Orin's memories. The last drop of the mixture in that jar was used five hundred years ago. There is no more."

No more, no more, whispered the echoes.

"Then the mixture must be made again," said Rowan, lifting his chin. "If they were Orin's hands I saw, the words I heard were his also."

"What words, Rowan?" urged Jonn.

The three Candidates leaned forward as one. Even cold Asha. Even withdrawn Doss.

"The recipe for the antidote," said Rowan.

He said the words aloud. He had no trouble remembering them. He felt as though they had been burnt into his brain.

"To mix the brew that wakes Death Sleep
Fill one spread hand with silver deep.
In hungry pool moons raise their heads:
Pluck one and add the tears it sheds.
Stir slowly with new fighter's quill,
Three times, no more, and let it still.
Add venom from your greatest fear—
One drop—and then the truth is clear."

Asha snorted.

"What ingredients are these?" muttered Seaborn.

Doss's eyes gleamed with interest. "Orin made a secret of his recipe," he said.

"Yes," said the Keeper. "And his secrets are mine." She turned to Rowan. "By Orin's will I cannot tell you how to read the rhyme," she said coldly. "But, believe me, even if I could tell you what the ingredients were, you would fail to obtain them. The antidote cannot be made."

"It can," said Rowan. "It must."

The Crystal glowed. Rowan felt a tug—a pulling at his mind. He fought it desperately.

"You cannot make me do your will, Keeper," he gasped. "You cannot change my mind. You are too weak."

"There is no time!" hissed the Keeper. "And what you plan is foolish, boy of Rin. If preparing the antidote was as simple a matter as you seem to think, I would have it here already, and your mother would be healing now. I am not a monster. I would cure her if I could. But the antidote to Death Sleep is made of things rare and almost impossible to obtain. You alone could never gain them, never—"

"He would not be alone," Strong Jonn broke in. "I would be with him."

He left Jiller's side and strode to the centre of the Cavern to stand beside Rowan. He towered over the Keeper. Compared with him she seemed as small and fragile as a child. But she shook her head, quite unafraid.

"By Orin's decree the Island is forbidden to all except the Keeper," she said. "And, at the time of the Choosing, the Chooser and the Candidates, who must be alone. You cannot go there, Jonn of the Orchard, on pain of death."

Jonn's mouth tightened. He turned to look at Jiller, still and pale, scarcely breathing. "There are things I fear more than my own death," he said.

"I, too," said the Keeper. "And one of them is breaking my trust. You cannot go to the Island, Jonn. I will prevent you. I still have power enough for that."

"So Rowan goes alone, by your will." Jonn's eyes were hard. "He goes alone, and we wait here. And you say he cannot succeed alone. So he does not succeed. Neither does he return to choose a new Keeper. So Jiller dies. And you die. And the Crystal dims, for ever. Is that not breaking your trust also?"

The Keeper smiled faintly. "You argue well, man of Rin. But you cannot go to the Island."

There was silence, broken only by the soft pattering of endlessly falling water.

Rowan saw what he must do. He needed help. He knew where he must take it. There was no choice. He looked at the three figures still standing behind the Keeper's chair. Masking the distrust and fear in his eyes, he spoke to them directly, for the first time.

"Asha of Umbray, Seaborn of Fisk, Doss of Pandellis. The Island is not forbidden to you. Will you help me?"

He had thought they would agree readily. After all, he was the Chooser. They would want to impress and please him. Each would want to convince him that it had not been they who had poisoned his mother.

But they hesitated, their eyes on the Keeper. They would not help him against her will.

She sat motionless, bent over the Crystal. Then, finally, she nodded.

"Very well," she said, her voice flat, expressionless. "What must be, must be. But I warn you. At sunrise, my life will end. And the Crystal will die with me, if the Choosing is not complete by then."

"I will return in time to finish the Choosing," whispered Rowan. "I promise."

"No doubt you mean what you say," said the Keeper. "You will return—if it is within your power. But the course you have decided to take is a dangerous one, Chooser. Dangerous for you, and for Maris, and for the whole of this land. Even now, perhaps, Zebak ships speed towards our shores. They will have had word of the dimming of the Crystal. They have spies everywhere."

"This is always a danger at the time of the Choosing," said Rowan through lips that suddenly seemed dry and stiff.

The Keeper looked at her hands, the webs transparent in the Crystal-light. "But only once before has the power of the Crystal itself been in such danger. Once before, three hundred years ago, when the Mirril perished. And then your ancestor, Lieth, accepted for your people the burden of the Choosing, and let the Crystal live for the good of all."

She raised her eyes. "You look very like Lieth, Rowan of Rin," she said. "Very, very like. It is strange to think that as he saved the Crystal's power, you may be the one who destroys it."

Rowan went cold. He glanced at Jonn, who was watching him gravely. Just for a moment his determination weakened. Then he looked at his mother, and knew that he was right.

Seaborn had been fidgeting restlessly. "Let us go," he urged. "Already the sun is on its downward path to the west. We should take advantage of the light."

Rowan turned to Jonn. "Will you see to Star while I am gone?" he asked.

Jonn nodded. Then he dug in his pocket and brought out a soft leather pouch. He tipped what it contained into his hand. It was a small, shining glass jar, with a gleaming silver top shaped like a flying fish skimming the waves.

"This was for Jiller," he said. "I had just bought it at the market when Perlain ran to me with the news of her illness. I thought it—beautiful. And therefore fit for her. Take it now, Rowan, and fill it with what will save her life. I can think of no better use for it."

His voice was strong and calm. But his work-hardened finger quivered as he gently touched the tiny silver fish before slipping the jar into its pouch once again, and handing it to Rowan.

Rowan put the pouch carefully into his own pocket.

He wanted to say something that would comfort Jonn, but he knew that anything he said would sound false. He could not promise that he would succeed in his quest. And he knew that whatever troubles and dangers he was about to face, they would be nothing to the pain Strong Jonn would suffer, waiting helplessly here.

"I will do my best, Jonn," he murmured. "My very best."

Jonn put a heavy hand on his shoulder. "I know you will," he said. "And my thoughts and hopes go with you."

Rowan turned away and walked to where the Candidates stood waiting for him.

"Are you not going to farewell your mother, Chooser of

Rin?" croaked the Keeper, watching him through slitted eyes as he passed her chair.

Rowan felt a surge of anger. And the anger gave him the courage to say the words he had not been able to say to Jonn. "No. I do not need to farewell my mother," he said, loudly enough for all to hear. "She will still be here, and alive, when I return with the antidote."

"We shall see," said the Keeper. "We shall see."

10 – The Island

They walked through the tunnel to the Island in silence and in single file. Rowan was leading. Asha, Doss and Seaborn had all stood back respectfully, waiting for him to enter the dark and dripping passage first.

Now they walked behind him, measuring their steps to his. Their soft shoes made no sound on the smooth, damp stones. Several times already Rowan had looked back, not sure that they were still following. But always they were there, three paces behind him, their eyes watchful.

They carried flaming torches to light their way. Shadows flickered eerily on the roof and walls of rock. Water gleamed where it seeped through cracks and trickled to the floor.

We are walking under the sea, Rowan kept thinking. The idea of that vast, moving weight of water above and around them made him shiver.

He turned his thoughts to the task ahead. In the Cavern of the Crystal he had been so intent on forcing the Keeper to open the way for him that he had not really had time to think. And since then, the strangeness of his journey under the sea had driven everything from his mind.

He had not yet tried to guess what Orin's riddling list

of ingredients might mean. He had not really considered the Keeper's warning that he had no hope of obtaining the ingredients, even if he knew what they were.

But now he thought of both these things. He wondered if the three Maris padding behind him were thinking of them too. Or were they too worried about the Crystal, and the Keeper, and themselves, and the delay they were all being forced to suffer, to think at all?

He saw a dim light ahead. The tunnel was ending. He realised that he could hear the sound of waves, too. A dull, distant crashing of water on the jagged rocks and cliffs of the Island.

"At the end of the tunnel there is a stair, Chooser of Rin."

It was Asha's voice, flat and cold.

Rowan turned to look at her. "Perhaps it would be better if you called me by my name," he said, trying to smile.

She did not smile back. "As you wish," she answered.

Rowan turned back towards the light at the end of the tunnel. Asha, at least, was not trying hard to please him, he thought. She was not pretending to be anything other than she was.

Perhaps that is what her trainers have told her to do, a voice in his head told him. Remember what Perlain said. The Candidates study the ways of Rin, so they will know how to please the Chooser. Perhaps Asha's trainers have told her that we of Rin despise pretence. So she plays the game of seeming to be honest with me while she schemes in secret. Who knows what she is really thinking?

He shook his head to drive the uncomfortable thought out. He wished he could trust the three people with him.

It would be hard enough for him to do what he had to do, without wondering all the time who was speaking the truth, and who was lying. Let alone who was a poisoner, and who was innocent.

At the end of the tunnel rose steep stone stairs, just as Asha had said. Daylight glimmered at the top.

Rowan began to climb. The sound of waves became louder with every step he took. The light grew stronger, streaming down through the bars of what seemed to be a gate.

He began to move faster, though by now he was panting, and his legs were aching. Whatever dangers the Island might hold for him, he was eager to breathe fresh air again, and see the sky above his head.

With relief he climbed the last few stairs, pushed open the rusting iron gate, and stumbled through it. His legs were trembling after the climb. He stood gasping, trying to catch his breath.

He had been so long underground that the daylight seemed blinding. His dazzled eyes watered so much that he could hardly see. He blinked furiously, wiping at them with the back of his hand. As his sight slowly returned to normal, he saw that he was standing on the Island's rocky shore. In front of him was thick forest, hung with vines.

He turned around to see Asha, Seaborn and Doss following him out into the open. The iron gate clanged shut behind them, screening off the stairs that seemed to fall away into darkness. Beyond, waves dashed themselves into foam on the rocks. And far away, across the choppy water, stretched the golden sand and rounded buildings of Maris.

Narrowing his eyes against the spray, Rowan searched the buildings, trying to pick out Star's stable. He knew Star would wonder where he was, when Jonn came in his place to fill her water bowl. She would miss him, and be unhappy.

On the beach children darted in and out of the waves, uncaring of the chill wind. Here and there men and women sat mending nets. A lone hooded figure, a woman dressed in the green of the Fisk clan, paced the shore.

For some reason she looked familiar. It was something about the way she was walking. Her arms were folded under her cape, and her back was very straight. Ah, of course. It was the stern Fisk woman who had been one of his guides to the Cavern of the Crystal.

Rowan became aware that someone was standing beside him, and slowly turned his head.

It was Seaborn. He did not know he was being observed. His face was grave, and his eyes were fixed on the beach.

What was he looking at? The children? The buildings? The people mending nets? Or was it the woman of Fisk he watched?

The woman on the beach stopped, turned, and faced the sea. She stood motionless. Her green cape whipped around her in the wind, the hood blowing back from her face.

She is looking at us, thought Rowan. He glanced again at Seaborn. He too was standing perfectly still, as though concentrating with all his strength. The salt spray beat against his face like rain, but he did not turn away or narrow his eyes against it as Rowan had had to do.

They do not move, or wave, or make any sign, thought

Rowan. But still she is sending him some sort of message from the Fisk. If they cannot read each other's thoughts, then the message is in how she stands. Or even that she has appeared on the beach at all. The plots and plans of these people are never-ending.

A fresh wave of anger rose in him, sticking in his throat. He felt as though he was choking with it.

He must have made some small sound, because Seaborn looked at him quickly, his face surprised and guilty

"Does your clan know already that the Choosing has been delayed?" Rowan asked bluntly. "Is that what her message is about?"

"Whose message? There is no message," said Seaborn, turning away.

But Rowan knew he was lying.

It's nothing but lies in this place, he thought bitterly. Lies twist in these people's minds like the serpents that coil under the surface of their sea.

Anger still boiled within him. He did not regret letting Seaborn know that he had not been fooled.

I do not have to watch my words, or pretend, with these people, he thought. Whatever else I have to fear, I do not have to fear death at their hands. The Keeper has told them that there is no time to send for another Chooser. None of the Candidates would risk the loss of the Crystal by killing me now.

And yet ... another thought suddenly rose and brushed against Rowan's mind like a slimy thing in the dark. Yet time had always been very short. The Keeper had called for the Choosing when it was already almost too late. The Candidates had known that from the start.

But Jiller had been poisoned. Delay in the Choosing was dangerous for Maris, yet delay had been caused.

The thought grew larger, stronger, and twisted itself into a question.

Why? Why would anyone with the fortunes of Maris at heart have done such a thing? What value would there be to a clan in winning the Choosing, if the Crystal was no more?

Rowan turned to look at the Candidates.

Seaborn had crouched to pull his shoe more tightly around his foot. Or so he pretended. His face was conveniently hidden. Asha and Doss stood apart from each other in the mist of spray—a tall silver figure, cape streaming back in the wind, a smaller figure in blue.

Rowan remembered Perlain's words.

The Candidates study the ways of Rin ... Their trainers know how you think. They have collected news of you since the day you were born.

If these strangers know me, know me truly, they could have guessed that I would not let my mother die without seeking help for her, thought Rowan. They could have guessed that I would delay the Choosing even further. Just as I have done.

His heart thudded. The thought was filling his mind now. He could see it face to face. And it was ugly and terrifying.

He had behaved just as someone had expected he would. He had been trapped into being part of someone's plan.

Someone wanted the Choosing to fail.

Someone wanted the Crystal's power to fade.

And they were using Rowan to help them do it.

11 – The Beginning

We have rested enough. We should delay no longer."

It was Asha's voice, stern and cold.

Rowan swallowed. He did not trust himself to speak. He pressed his hands together, trying to stop them from shaking.

"What is the matter?" asked Seaborn sharply. "Are you ill?"

Rowan felt, rather than saw, the Candidates exchange quick, suspicious glances.

"I am not ill," he forced himself to say.

He drew a shuddering breath, and tried to calm his mind. He thought of Star, of Jonn, of Annad at home in Rin. Of his mother lying dreaming in the Cavern of the Crystal.

Nothing has really changed, he said to himself. Whoever is behind this wickedness, and whatever their reasons are, I must do what I came to do. I must follow Orin's directions. I must make the antidote to Death Sleep. And quickly.

In his pocket was the glass jar Jonn had given him, nestled in its soft leather pouch. He pulled the jar out and looked at it. A beautiful, shining thing, but empty. Waiting to be filled with what would save his mother's life.

He held the jar in his hand and repeated Orin's verse in a low voice.

> *"To mix the brew that wakes Death Sleep*
> *Fill one spread hand with silver deep.*
> *In hungry pool moons raise their heads:*
> *Pluck one and add the tears it sheds.*
> *Stir slowly with new fighter's quill,*
> *Three times, no more, and let it still.*
> *Add venom from your greatest fear—*
> *One drop—and then the truth is clear."*

"These words make no sense to me," said Seaborn.

"They are Orin's words," said Asha harshly. "They are secret words, not intended to be understood by others. For a thousand years they have been hidden. It is wrong to go against Orin's will. So it has always been."

Doss hesitated. "The first line is simple," he began finally. "But the second ... 'silver deep' ..."

"The second is simple also," said Seaborn impatiently. "To begin the brew we must take a handful of water from the deep. From the sea."

Asha looked scornful. "The first two lines a child could understand," she said. "It is not they that are the problem."

Rowan unscrewed the lid of the jar. His fingers shook. Do not listen to their squabbling, he said to himself. Think only about what you are doing. Get the water. The first ingredient. Make a start.

He moved away from the Candidates, and walked quickly through the mist of spray towards the rocky edge of the Island.

"Wait, Chooser of Rin," he heard Asha call.

Rowan kept walking. He was angry. You want me to fail in this, Asha, he raged at her in his mind. You have tried to discourage me. But you will not.

He reached the rocks and began to clamber from one to the other, down towards the sea.

It was then, as his anger died, that he saw his danger. The waves flung themselves against the Island, breaking into clouds of spray and sheets of hissing foam. His heavy shoes slipped on the wet, glass-smooth rocks. It was like walking on ice. As he edged closer to the water, chill spray rained on his head and beat into his face, stinging his eyes, blinding him.

His stomach lurched as a wave struck and his right foot slipped from under him. He cried out, struggling desperately to regain his balance. Before his streaming eyes the world tilted crazily ...

Then three pairs of hands were catching at his arms, pulling him back, steadying him. He turned, gasping, to see the faces of Seaborn, Asha and Doss looking at him gravely.

Rowan felt sick. He had so nearly fallen. His head would have struck the iron-hard rocks. The waves would have sucked him into the cold, churning sea.

The Candidates had all moved to save him. Could it be, then, that he had been wrong? That he did not have an enemy among them?

Or was it just that it was not yet time for him to die? Did someone need him alive, and wasting precious moments, till the Keeper finally slid away from the shores of life and the Crystal dimmed for ever?

Rowan blinked at the three faces before him, and wiped his eyes. "Thank you," he said dully.

Seaborn smiled. "Your shoes are not made for rock-walking, Rowan."

"I told you to wait," said Asha severely. "You must let us swim the dangerous waters, if they are to be swum at all."

"I asked you to help me," Rowan mumbled. "But I do not expect you to risk your lives."

Asha's lips made a straight, hard line. "The death of one of us is of no account," she said. "But if you are lost, the whole of Maris is lost also."

Seaborn nodded. "Give me the jar, and I will fetch the water," he said. "We should waste no more time."

Doss opened his mouth as if to say something, then seemed to change his mind. His eyes, so strangely dreamy for a Maris, slid from Rowan's face to the boiling sea.

"What is it?" Rowan asked him.

"I—I do not believe this water fits the words of the rhyme," said Doss. "I think we must look in another place."

The others stared.

"The sea is the deep," said Asha.

"And all shines silver in the sun," said Seaborn.

Doss shook his head. "The words 'silver deep' are still, and quiet, and full of mystery," he said. "But in this place the sea is wild. It fights the land. It churns itself into foam. I do not think Orin would have called it the silver deep."

"Who are you to know the mind of Orin?" snapped Asha.

Doss looked at the ground and did not answer.

Rowan bit his lip. Slowly he screwed the silver top

back on the jar. Now that he thought about it, he could see that Doss was right.

He felt sick with disgust at his own foolishness. He had let anger and fear drive him. He had forgotten how cunning were the Maris folk—and the great Orin more than any. He had been desperate, and far too willing to believe that Orin's first ingredient could be so simple to find.

He had been so unthinking, indeed, that he had nearly lost his life by rushing to collect something which would have proved useless.

I must be more careful, he thought. I must panic no more. I must be as cold as these Maris, if I am to outwit them.

He took a deep breath.

"What do you think the silver deep is, Doss?" he asked quietly.

"I do not know," murmured Doss. "But it must be here. On or around the Island. Because it is here that Orin made his brew."

"We will search, then. Search until we find it." Rowan stuffed the jar back into his pocket, and looked around him. Rocky shore, crashing waves, tufted grass, wild, tangled forest ... Where should they begin?

He repeated the question aloud. "Where should we begin?"

Seaborn's voice rose above the sound of the waves. "The Island is like unknown waters, to us," he said. "None but the Keeper may visit here, except at the time of the Choosing. But often I have sailed around it. And on the other side, the side you cannot see from Maris, there are quiet, sandy bays and sheltered places. Perhaps there ..."

Rowan considered this, then nodded. "We will try," he said. "We will go around the shore. It will not take long. Better that than try to break through the forest."

"If we go to the other side of the Island we will be hidden from Maris," murmured Asha. "And the Crystal is too dim for the Keeper's mind to follow us. If any danger befalls us on the secret side, there will be no help."

"We will have to depend on each other for help," said Rowan.

As the words left his lips he saw the three Candidates again exchange suspicious looks, frown, and touch the knives at their belts.

Despair settled over him. There was little chance that the Candidates of Fisk, Pandellis and Umbray would depend on one another. For them, at this time, no enemy was more dangerous than one of their own kind.

He began to pick his way along the shore, keeping close to the trees, and as far away as possible from the treacherous rocks.

Asha's words came back to him. Whatever happened on the other side of the Island would not be seen from Maris. He would be quite unprotected. There would be nothing to stop one of the three Candidates from killing him. Whoever it was could kill the others too, then return to the Keeper with the story that they had all fallen by accident into the sea.

Was this journey, too, part of someone's plan?

12 – Out of Sight

Rowan felt lonely and afraid. If only I could talk to someone I know I can trust, he thought.

He glanced behind him. The Candidates were following in single file. Asha, her silver cape reflecting the trees and the sea in turn, was first, gliding along very close to him.

Rowan suddenly realised why she seemed so familiar. Despite her strange looks and clothes, Asha reminded him of Jiller, his mother. She seemed strictly honest, stern, straightforward, determined to do what was right, whatever the cost.

He faced forward again, and moved on. They were rounding the Island now. Soon the Maris shore would be lost to sight.

His thoughts ran on. Yes, Asha reminded him of his mother. Despite his anger at her lack of encouragement, it made him want to trust her. He remembered that Asha was the one who had sounded the warning about the Island's secret side.

But she knew I would not hesitate because of that, he thought. Knew, perhaps, that it would make me all the more determined.

Their trainers know how you think.

I must not forget that, Rowan told himself. I must never forget it.

He turned his thoughts to Seaborn, who was striding behind Asha, tall and solid in green. Seaborn was energetic, confident and strong. A man who could be depended upon. He reminded Rowan of Jonn—Strong Jonn, who had so often helped him and stood beside him in times of danger.

It was Seaborn who had suggested going to the secret side of the Island. He had seemed to suggest it only because he was eager to help. Keen for action, as Jonn would have been.

But was he? Or was he simply carrying out the next step in a plot?

Rowan shook his head. He could not be sure of Seaborn either.

So—Doss. Doss was last in the line. He was so much smaller than the others that all Rowan had been able to see of him was a flickering blue shape appearing briefly and then disappearing behind Seaborn's green.

Doss was quiet and dreamy, and more uncertain than the others. Did Doss remind Rowan of anyone?

Yes, of course he did. Doss was like Rowan himself. Surely, then, he was the one to trust.

Yet it was Doss who had raised doubts about the silver deep. It was his seemingly hesitant words that had led finally to this journey, though Doss himself had not suggested it.

Was Doss in fact the cleverest and most dangerous of all?

Rowan's mind spun. Nothing was certain. He was drifting helplessly in swirling tides of questions and confusion. He slid his hand into his pocket and gripped the silver-topped jar, drawing comfort from its solid hardness.

I can trust none of them, he thought. I can trust only myself.

Suddenly he became aware that he was walking on sand, instead of rock. He looked up and discovered that while he had been thinking, he had rounded the Island's curve without noticing it.

As Seaborn had said, the other side of the Island was a sheltered bay. The trees beside him were no longer a solid mass. Instead, dim, ferny trails wound away into the forest depths, and he could see grassy clearings through the vines and trunks.

Gentler waves broke and foamed on this softer, curving shore. At the other end of the beach a high, jagged cliff rose from the sea like a barrier. Around it, two large birds swooped and called harshly. They were the only sign of life.

Beyond the waves, as far as the eye could see, there was nothing but sea and sky.

Now, thought Rowan, I am truly alone. He forced his mind away from his fear.

Silver deep ...

Rowan looked along the line of waves rolling into the shore. They were smaller than the waves on the other side of the Island, certainly. But still they did not seem to match the words.

He felt a prickling at the back of his neck, and spun around to see Asha, Seaborn and Doss standing close behind him. They had caught up to him and were waiting.

How long had they been there? He couldn't say. They moved so silently.

I must tell them what we are going to do next, thought Rowan. And again despair swept over him.

I am not a leader, he thought. I do not know where to turn next. I am a stranger here. I am afraid. I have insisted on doing this thing, and now I do not know where to go or what to do.

He looked again at the three Candidates. And slowly he realised that they seemed different.

Just a couple of hours ago, he would not have seen it. But since then he had become used to seeing Maris faces. They had stopped looking alike to him. He had started to notice expressions and changes of mood in those he spoke to.

Now he saw that Asha, Seaborn and Doss were afraid. Their eyes were wary. They were standing stiffly, holding themselves ready for danger. Their hands hovered close to the knives on their belts.

On this side of the Island they are as much strangers as I am, he thought. They have not studied this place. They cannot see their home. They have never set foot on this sand before. They do not know what they will find here.

For some reason, the thought helped him.

"I think we should start by walking along the sand," he said aloud. "Look left and right, for anything that fits the words."

"The deep is the sea," said Asha, behind him. "We will not find it among trees, Chooser of Rin."

"Deep has more meanings than one," said Doss in a low voice. "The rhyme does not say '*the* silver deep', but 'silver deep' only."

"What difference does that make?" the woman retorted. "It is clear what Orin meant."

Seaborn laughed. "Who are *you*, Asha of Umbray, to know the mind of Orin?" he jeered.

"Watch your slimy tongue, Fisk!" spat Asha.

"Watch your own," said Seaborn.

Rowan said nothing. He felt like shouting at them. He felt like begging them to work together, to help him. But he knew it would be no use.

He trudged along, knowing that they would follow. The sand squeaked under his feet. As he walked, he looked from sea to forest and back again.

His heart sank as the minutes passed.

Nothing. He could see nothing.

Not too far ahead, the sand ended at the foot of the high, rocky cliff that stretched across the beach and jutted far into the sea. Once they reached that, they could go no further. The only place left to search would be the forest itself. And though the Island was small, with no clues to guide them such a search could take days.

If only I knew what I was looking for, Rowan thought desperately. He passed yet another gap in the trees, peered into it, saw waving plumes of tall, spiky grass, and moved on.

One of the birds he had heard before screeched from the forest depths. He glanced towards the sound. And then, as he began to turn his head back to the sea, he saw something. Just a flash, glimpsed from the corner of his eye.

He stopped dead, and took a pace back. He peered through the trees. Yes, there it was again. Somewhere in the green depths there was a glint of silver. Like still, secret water, touched briefly by the sun.

"I think—there's something in there," he said, pointing. He tried to speak calmly, but his heart was thudding with excitement.

Somehow he knew without doubt that he had at last found Orin's silver deep.

13 – Silver Deep

They pushed through the tall grass, and crept cautiously into the forest. For a moment they hesitated, wondering and silent.

The trees rose high on either side of them. Leafy branches, locked together, made a roof over their heads, blocking out the sun. And now that they were beyond the tall grass, they could see that they were standing on a wide path that wound deep into the forest.

Rowan saw Doss shiver as he looked around.

"Who has made this?" Seaborn wondered aloud.

For it was certain that the path had not come about by chance. It was flat and wide—wide enough for the four of them to walk easily side by side. It was edged by high banks of earth that had been pushed aside and then completely overgrown by bushes, moss and ferns.

"It must be the Keeper," said Asha. "For only the Keeper is permitted on the Island. But clearly the path has not been used for a long time."

She pointed at the thick layer of rotting leaves that covered the trail, and the clusters of ferns that uncurled tender fronds here and there.

Rowan nodded. "At least a year," he said. "If these plants grow as they do in Rin."

"Nevertheless," Seaborn said grimly, "we should be on the watch for danger."

They moved forward, their feet sinking into the brown, leafy carpet. Fat grey moths fluttered blindly into their path, brushing their faces with soft wings.

Rowan strained his eyes in the dimness, searching the way ahead for another glint of silver.

Through the trees he saw a flash of brighter green, and heard again the fierce squawking of one of the birds he had seen swooping near the cliff.

It doesn't sound too friendly, he thought. An idea stirred in his mind, but immediately excitement swept it aside. For suddenly, just ahead, while the bird call was still dying away, the silver he was seeking gleamed again.

"There," he gasped. He began to run.

He could hear Asha, Seaborn and Doss hurrying behind him. For once they were having more trouble than he. Their light shoes sank into the softness of the path, slowing them down.

A smell of damp and earth rose from the leaves as they were trampled beneath his feet. It mixed with the other scents of the forest. Fresh leaves, bruised ferns, mould ... and something else.

Rowan's nose twitched as he tried to make out what the something else was. It was a heavy, sweet perfume. Some forest flower, perhaps, but like nothing he had ever smelt in Rin. And it was growing stronger.

The path curved slightly, then opened out into what seemed to be a natural clearing, ringed by trees. Leaves and grass covered the earth around the edge of the clearing, but in the centre rose a smooth, bare brown rock, folded and curved, like a huge, huddled animal sleeping.

The sky made a pale circle overhead, lighting the clearing. The rough cliff towered grey above the treetops on one side.

There was no wind. No noise, except the distant sound of the sea. It was a still, secret place. On the rock, puddles of water gleamed.

"There must be a pool up there," Rowan whispered. "A spring, fed from a stream under the rock."

There was no reason to whisper. But Rowan's skin was prickling. He sensed danger.

Perhaps it was the light, after the dimness of the forest. Perhaps it was the strange, sweet smell that was suddenly all around him. Or perhaps it was the silence of the place, and the strangeness of it.

Asha, Seaborn and Doss, too, seemed to have been struck dumb. Rowan only knew they were behind him because he could hear them breathing.

He stepped on to the rock. They followed as he slowly climbed to the top.

And there, just as he had hoped, was a deep pool of crystal-clear water, cupped in the rock. It was almost perfectly round, and so small that two people could touch hands across it.

Far below the surface, silver gleamed. The bottom of the pool was covered in some sort of shining mud or sand.

But this was not what made Rowan gasp, and his heart fill with hope. There was something else under that clear, rippling surface. Something round and white, shining through the water like a full moon floating in the sky.

It was a flower. Its face was turned to the sky, the petals fanning out to make a perfect circle. Rowan could smell its perfume rising from the water. The heavy, sweet scent he had noticed before.

In hungry pool moons raise their heads ...

"Flowers cannot grow under water," exclaimed Asha, shocked out of her silence.

She sounded almost angry, because the laws she had thought to be fixed had been overturned. For Asha, flowers grew in the air and sun. That was how it had always been. That was how it always must be.

But Seaborn's face was alive with curiosity and excitement. "This one does," he said. "And it is the second ingredient. We have found two in one place! Quickly, Rowan. The water, and then the flower."

Rowan pulled the glass jar from his pocket and unscrewed the lid.

Fill one spread hand with silver deep ...

He spread his hand, bent to the water, looked at his fingers, hesitated ...

"Wait," breathed Doss, touching his arm. "Remember—"

Rowan barely heard him. He was staring, fascinated, at the water. For suddenly the moon flower was disappearing from sight. The pool was no longer clear. It was turning silver as he watched.

He turned to Seaborn, to tell him. And in that instant he saw the man's face change, felt himself being roughly pulled to the ground.

"Beware!" yelled Seaborn.

A terrible, piercing cry split the air. Great wings beat

above their heads. There was a splash. Water flowed out onto the rock.

And then a huge green bird was flying away, soaring back to its cliff-top, several small, wriggling fish clutched in its claws. Rowan had never seen such a bird. It was as big as he was.

Seaborn snorted with shaken laughter. "I thought it was attacking us. But it was only intent on filling its belly! And the bellies of its young. No wonder Orin called this 'hungry pool'."

Doss began to speak, but his voice was drowned out by Asha. She had scrambled to her feet, and was pointing fearfully at the pool.

"That light!" she called. "What is it?"

Rowan crawled back to the edge of the pool. The perfume of the flower was very strong. And the water looked like melted silver. Silver as Asha's cloak. Silver as sunlight striking water. Silver as a fish. He could hardly look at it, so brightly was it flashing in the sun.

In an instant he realised what had happened. The fish, diving for safety from the bird, had stirred up the shining sand at the bottom of the pool.

Fill one spread hand with silver deep ...

"Seaborn!" he yelled. "Quickly! Before the silver sinks again. Take a handful of the water!"

Seaborn hesitated, puzzled.

"My hand will not do," shouted Rowan. "I realised it just before the bird struck. Spread, my hand is useless. The rhyme means a Maris hand. With webbed fingers, like Orin's."

Seaborn nodded, and sprang to Rowan's side.

"*No!*" cried Doss.

But already Seaborn had scooped his spread hand through the water.

He began to lift it out again. Rowan readied the jar to collect the water. Then suddenly Seaborn screamed in agony.

He jerked his hand into the air. Silver liquid brimmed from the wide cup made by his spread fingers. But the whole of the back of his hand and his wrist were covered by dozens of wriggling fish. Even out of the water they were still biting into the flesh, then dropping back into the pool covered in pale Maris blood.

Asha shrieked with disgust and horror.

"Hungry pool ..." murmured Doss.

"Rowan, the jar," shouted Seaborn, shuddering with pain. "Oh, quickly, for Orin's sake! They are eating me alive!"

Wordlessly Rowan thrust the container towards him. With his free hand Seaborn gripped his injured wrist, steadying it, and tipped the precious silver liquid into the jar.

Fish were still falling from his flesh. His blood was dripping freely into the pool. And the pool was swarming, seething, as the fish feasted.

Groaning, Seaborn staggered back. He plucked the last of the squirming creatures from his hand and threw it to the rock. He swayed. His face was as pale as the underbelly of a fish.

Rowan ran to his side, and helped him to sit, and then to lie back on the ground. Gently he turned over the small webbed hand. Only then was the full horror of the injuries revealed.

The fish had truly been trying to strip the flesh from Seaborn's bones. The wounds were terrible.

"In my supplies," gasped Seaborn. "Healing cream. Bandages."

Asha and Doss came closer as Rowan pulled a jar of sticky brown ointment and a roll of soft, silky bandage from a pouch sewn into Seaborn's cape.

"I will help you," said Asha, reaching for the bandage.

"No!" Seaborn cried feebly, clutching with his good hand at Rowan's jacket. "Rowan! Do not let them touch me! Do not let them near my supplies!"

Asha drew back. "I would not try to harm you, man of Fisk," she frowned. "It is forbidden. And in any case, there is no need. You have done enough harm to yourself, without my doing more."

Rowan began to smear the brown ointment on Seaborn's hand. He was as gentle as he could be, but Seaborn closed his eyes, his face twisted in pain.

"If Seaborn is injured, it is my fault," Rowan muttered. "The pool was rippling, yet there was no wind. I took no note of that. And even when I saw the bird take the fish from the water, I did not think of danger. I did not heed the warning in Orin's rhyme."

He looked up at Doss. "You did," he added. "You tried to tell me. I wish that I had listened to you."

"I wish that I had spoken more firmly," said Doss. "But I was not certain. It was an idea only." He gazed thoughtfully down at Seaborn's white face.

Now that the crisis had passed, Doss was as calm as ever. He did not seem particularly upset by Seaborn's distress. Even for a Maris, he was strangely unmoved.

Rowan wondered about this as he bent to bandage the groaning man's quivering hand. Was Doss secretly glad that Seaborn had been injured? Had he deliberately held his tongue until his warning was too late?

Or was it just that Doss had seen so much pain and death in his life that he was no longer moved by it?

There is so much about these people I do not know, thought Rowan. When it comes to the Choosing, how will I decide which of these Candidates will best rule Maris?

He tried to turn his mind away from the question. The important thing now was the cure for Jiller. That came first.

One ingredient for the antidote had been found. Now the second had to be added.

In hungry pool moons raise their heads:
Pluck one and add the tears it sheds.

Just a few minutes ago, that task had seemed easy. Plunge an arm into that clear, rippling water. Pick the flower growing deep within it.

But now ... who would risk such a thing?

No one.

14 – Hungry Pool

Rowan finished bandaging Seaborn's hand, and helped him to sit upright while he bound his arm into a sling. He saw the man gaze with loathing at the fish, now lying still on the rock where it had fallen.

Now they could all see clearly its transparent, worm-like body, and the swollen head that seemed just big enough to hold its double row of needle-sharp teeth.

"Never have I seen such a thing!" breathed Asha. "And there are thousands of them."

She climbed the rock and stood staring down at the pool.

"It is clear again," she said.

Rowan went to look.

Sure enough, the pool shone clean and clear. The silver sand had sunk once again to the bottom. There was no trace of Seaborn's blood, either. The fish, it seemed, had made short work of that.

The moon-flower floated temptingly in the rippling depths. It looked as though you could reach down and pick it—easily, easily. And just a few minutes ago, Rowan had thought he could.

"We will have to break the flower's stem with two

sticks and lift it from the water," Asha suggested.

Rowan shook his head. "I do not think we can do that," he said. "The rhyme says we must add the tears the flower sheds. I think the tears must be the juice that drips from the broken stem. If we simply break the stem from above, it will flow to waste in the water. The flower must be picked by hand, and the stem pinched hard to hold the juice in place."

One of the grey moths from the forest bumbled over the pool, attracted by the scent of the flower. The water rippled. Perfume rose from its surface in waves of sweetness. The moth flew lower. Its wing just touched the water …

In a blink, it had disappeared below the surface. The water seethed and swirled as though it was boiling. And then there was nothing.

Rowan shuddered. He fought down the sickness that churned his stomach.

It is the way of the world, he told himself. The fish eat the moths. The bird eats the fish. So it goes.

But still, the death of the helpless moth had upset him.

"If a few moths are all those creatures have to eat, it is a wonder they are so many," Asha commented, unmoved.

Rowan swallowed, and nodded. "Somehow, we have to find a way to deal with them," he said. "Somehow, we have to pick the moon-flower."

"There is only one way to deal with fish," said Asha firmly. "Even fish as extraordinary as these. We will catch them. Net them, every one."

"I do not think we have a net that will hold them," called Doss, overhearing.

Asha faced him, wrapping her silver cape around her. "We do not have a single net fine enough, it's true," she retorted. "But if we lay all our nets together, so that the lines of the mesh cross one another, the web will do. I am sure of it."

Doss glanced at the sky. "You had better move away from the pool," he said urgently. "The bird is coming back."

Remembering what had happened last time, Rowan and Asha hastily moved further down the rock.

Rowan turned to look. The bird swooped down towards the pool at enormous speed. It was huge. Its beak was cruel and curved. Its claws were stretched out, glinting, ready to grasp its prey.

As Rowan watched, the bird hovered for a moment over the pool. The water began to turn silver as the fish scurried to safety.

And then, suddenly, the bird swerved in the air, and with a harsh cry headed straight for Rowan and Asha.

"Down!" shrieked Rowan, pushing Asha to the ground.

Just in time. The snapping beak, the beating wings and razor-sharp claws missed them both by the tiniest space.

Rowan stared in amazement as the bird wheeled away.

"What—what is it doing?" cried Seaborn.

"I don't know," panted Rowan. "It seems to have decided that we are its enemies."

Asha climbed to her feet, pale and shaken.

"I will be glad to leave this place," she said. She pulled a fine net from the pouch in her cape. "And to this end," she added, "I would ask the Candidates of Pandellis and of Fisk to give me their nets, so I can clear the pool."

Without a word, Seaborn plucked at his own cape with

his uninjured hand, and brought out a net even finer than Asha's. He held it out.

Doss hesitated, then did the same.

Asha spread all three nets out on the rock, one on top of the other, and tied the edges in many places. Rowan could see that, joined together, the nets made a fine web. There were very few spaces through which fish might escape, even fish as small as those in the pool.

Asha stood up with the three nets made one in her hand. She glanced at the cliff-top beyond the trees. The green bird was shrieking there, beating its wings at one of its own kind which had dared to enter its territory.

"Our friend is busy for the moment," she said. "Now is our chance."

She carried the net to the moon-flower pool, and knelt beside it. Rowan and Doss ran to help her. They crouched around the pool, holding the net between them.

"We must dip the net, lift the fish out, tip them onto the rock where they cannot harm us, and dip again as quickly as we can," Asha said. "It will take time to empty the pool completely."

She looked behind her at Seaborn, who was watching helplessly, nursing his injured hand. "Warn us if the bird approaches," she ordered. "No doubt you will be pleased to have something useful to do."

She turned back to Rowan and Doss. It suits her to be the one in charge, thought Rowan.

"Ready?" said Asha. "Now!"

They dipped the net into the pool. The water seethed. Rowan felt a slight tug at his hands. He tensed his muscles, ready to lift ...

"Out!" called Asha.

They lifted together. Rowan had expected a small weight—but there was no weight at all.

He rocked back on his heels, staring stupidly at the ragged piece of net he held. He looked up at the others. They, too, were blinking, as though they couldn't take in what had happened.

The entire centre of the net had disappeared. And in the pool, the fish feasted.

"Never—" Asha was trembling with shock and anger. "Never have I seen anything like this. What devils are these?"

The water was calming. Soon it was gently rippling once more, and they could again see the moon-flower blooming. There was no sign of the net, or any part of it. It had been completely consumed.

"I do not believe it!" Asha shouted. "They eat our net, yet they do not eat the flower!"

"I think I see why," said Doss. "It is because they need the flower. Its perfume attracts the moths that they often use for food." He smiled. "And of course," he added, "the flower needs the fish also. They eat whatever falls into the pool, so the water stays clear and clean, and the flower can always see the sun."

"Beware!" cried Seaborn.

They scrambled away from the pool, staying low.

The green-feathered bird swooped down. The pool began to turn silver. The bird plunged, then rose, screeching, clutching wriggling prey.

"The bird can take the fish," said Doss slowly.

"It has been fitted by nature to do so!" snapped Asha.

"And we cannot wait for it to empty the pool for us."

"Do we have a container with which we can take the water out?" asked Seaborn.

No one did. And after what had happened to the net, they all knew that a container made of leaves, cloth or bark would be useless.

"I have it! We will fill the pool with sand and rocks," said Asha, jumping up. "Then the water will overflow and run away, and the devil-fish will die."

"We have no time to waste. It would take many, many hours to fill that pool," murmured Seaborn. "And I—" He winced, nursing his injured hand. "I will be able to help you little."

"It does not matter!" Asha's pale eyes were burning with anger. "Those creatures must be destroyed. They must!"

Rowan shook his head. "You are forgetting," he said gently. "Our aim is not to destroy the fish. Our aim is to pluck the moon-flower. If we fill the pool, the flower will be buried deep. It will be damaged, perhaps broken. Then it will be useless."

Asha threw up her hands. "We must destroy the fish before we can pick the flower!" she raged. "If we cannot destroy them, the thing cannot be done!"

"Yes, it can," cried Rowan. "It must."

"It can be done," said Doss. "Because Orin did it. There is a way. We have only to find it."

There was silence. They crouched on the rock, watching as the great green bird once more swooped to the pool, hovered for a second while the water silvered under its shadow, then plunged.

"The fish are afraid of the bird," said Doss suddenly.

"They rush to bury themselves beneath the silver sand just before it swoops. And there they stay until the danger has passed."

"You are thinking that at that moment we could pluck the flower in safety," Rowan murmured.

Seaborn looked doubtful. "It all happens in the blink of an eye," he said. "And there are still fish in the water, for the bird always catches some. But we could try, and hope that there are too few to do too much damage."

Asha snorted. "You dream, you three, if you think of standing in the way of that bird as it attacks. It would be madness. You would be cut to pieces."

She looked up to the cliff-top, where the bird was again fighting with one of its own kind. Green feathers fell to the sea below as it beat its wings in fury, its curved claws slashing at the intruder.

Rowan nodded. The bird was in its way as dangerous as the ravenous fish. And in any case, Seaborn's objection, too, was serious. The moment of safety, while the bird hovered, was too fleeting. Even the fish did not all have time to scatter and bury themselves in the silver sand.

But they all tried. Because they knew they were in danger. Like the cornbirds that scattered from the grain fields in Rin when someone approached. Or when Jiller placed a ...

Rowan caught his breath.

"What is it?" asked Doss.

"I know what to do," said Rowan. "I need a knife. And Seaborn's cloak. And some long, straight sticks."

15 – The Plan

he green bird had plunged to the pool many times before Rowan's work was finished.

"In Orin's name, please hurry," Seaborn urged him, glancing restlessly at the sun.

Rowan bit his lip, forcing himself to concentrate on what he was doing. He knew only too well that time was precious. And yet the work had to be done properly, or it would fail.

Finally he tied the last knots, and stood back.

Asha, Doss and Seaborn stared silently at the thing Rowan had made. It was a bird shape, cut roughly from part of Seaborn's green cloak, and stiffened with sticks like a kite.

Seaborn frowned. "It is a curious idea," he said. "How did you think of it?"

"My mother makes a figure from wood and dresses it in her clothes, to scare the cornbirds from our fields," said Rowan, lifting the shape in his arms.

"But it will not fool the devil-fish, surely," said Asha.

"I hope it might," said Rowan. "In Rin, the trick does not work for cornbirds that are old and wise. But it scares away those that have not yet learned how to tell real danger from false. And I believe these fish are like those young cornbirds. For if I am right, no one has tried this trick here since Orin's time."

He carried the shape to the pool, and scanned the skies. The green bird was nowhere to be seen.

"Now is the time," he said, beckoning. "Quickly, before the real bird returns, or the sun sets. It is important that the shadow of the bird shape falls on the surface of the water."

Doss and Asha stood back from the pool and took the shape between them, holding it by the edges of its wings.

Rowan lay down beside the pool, his eyes fixed on the moon-flower. Seaborn, wincing with pain as he moved, crouched beside him, holding the glass jar.

In hungry pool moons raise their heads:
Pluck one ...

"Now," Rowan murmured.

Asha and Doss moved forward, one on either side of the pool. The shadow of the bird shape they held between them fell over the water.

Immediately, the pool began to cloud, and then to shine. The fish were burrowing for their lives beneath the silver sand.

"Wait ... wait," Doss whispered. "Let them all go."

Rowan's hand tingled. He counted to five, slowly. And then he knew he could wait no longer. Gritting his teeth, he plunged his arm into the cold, silvery depths. Down, down ... every second expecting the piercing pain that would signal that the ravenous fish had emerged from hiding, realising they had been tricked.

The stem of the moon-flower was between his fingers, smooth and hard. He bent it, but it did not break.

"Make haste!" Seaborn begged.

Desperately Rowan leaned further over the pool and plunged his other arm into the water, tearing at the moon-flower stem with his nails. The silver water lapped at his chest, his neck, his chin. If the fish were to attack now ...

He felt the stem break. Pinching the end with the fingers of one hand, holding the flower with the other, he wriggled backwards, grazing himself on the rocks. And just as the white flower broke the surface of the water, blazing pain shot through his forearms and wrists.

He heard Asha and Seaborn shouting in horror. He smelled the heavy, overwhelming scent of the already wilting flower. He looked down at his arms, where a dozen transparent, biting creatures hung, wriggling.

His mind was clouded by pain that was like a thousand needles. But Seaborn was holding out the glass jar, calling to him.

Pluck one and add the tears it sheds ...

Rowan thrust the stem of the flower over the jar, and loosened his pinching fingers.

... add the tears it sheds.

And precious drops were falling into the jar. Mixing with the silver liquid. Turning it blue. Blue as the shining cloth of Doss's cloak. Blue as the sea. Blue as the sky.

* * *

"There. It is done," said Doss, fastening the last bandage.

Rowan thanked him. His arms still throbbed and ached. But the sticky brown ointment and the bandages were comforting.

He looked over to the rock where the moon-flower lay broken and already yellowing. He felt sorry that it had to die.

Doss followed his glance, and gave one of his rare smiles. "Come," he said, beckoning. Rowan stood up and followed him.

The pool was rippling and clear. And far below its surface glimmered the perfect white face of another moon-flower.

"There was a bud beneath the bloom you picked," Doss said, as Rowan gasped. "It opened the moment the pool cleared. I saw it happen. It was like a miracle."

"A miracle!" exclaimed Asha, coming up beside them. "How can you call a thing so evil a miracle?"

Doss turned serious eyes towards her. "The flower is not evil because it blooms where it does," he said. "It simply exists. As do the fish in this pool, and the bird on the cliff, and you, and I."

Asha returned his look coldly. "You never forget that you are the Candidate, do you, Doss of Pandellis?" she sneered. "And how well you have studied this Chooser! You say exactly what will please him."

Doss frowned. "I do not," he said. "I say what I think."

She laughed disbelievingly, and went to sit by herself at the edge of the rock.

Rowan looked quickly at Doss, then away again. He was thrilling with shock. He had suddenly realised he had let down his guard.

For a while he had actually forgotten that his companions were not his friends, or even his willing helpers. He had forgotten what Perlain had told him: that they had been trained from earliest childhood to be cunning, and to please the Chooser, whatever their true thoughts.

He had forgotten that one of them had poisoned his mother.

But now he remembered, and his anger returned. He lifted his head, ignoring the throbbing pain of his arms, and the even greater ache in his heart.

"We must find the third ingredient," he said loudly, avoiding all their eyes.

"Stir slowly with new fighter's quill,
Three times, no more, and let it still."

The calm, strong voice that said the words was Seaborn's.

"I believe I have the third ingredient already, Rowan," he said. He held up a long green feather. "The bird plucked this from its own wing, in rage, when it was attacking Asha."

Rowan thought quickly. A quill was a feather. That was true. The bird could be called a fighter. That was true. The other two ingredients had been found here, in this place. It was very likely that the third would be also.

And the fourth?

Rowan shut his eyes. He would not think of the fourth. He had never wanted to think of the fourth.

He held out his hand, and Seaborn put the feather into it. They saw the bird coming towards them again, and jumped aside. But the bird paid no attention to them. It simply splashed into the pool as before, and flew away.

Rowan unscrewed the lid of the jar. He put the sharp

end of the green feather into the blue liquid and stirred. Once, twice, three times.

Nothing happened.

The rhyme says, "let it still", he thought. He set the jar upon the rock and watched its contents carefully.

Slowly the liquid settled, and became still. But the colour remained unchanged.

Rowan willed himself to say nothing. He turned the feather around, forced its broad end into the neck of the jar, and stirred the mixture again. Then once more he moved back, to watch and wait.

After two long minutes, he knew he could wait no longer. Slowly he screwed the top back on the jar.

All three Candidates were watching him curiously. They could see that something was wrong, but they did not understand what the problem was.

"The mixture should have turned green," Rowan told them. He tried to speak strongly, like a leader. But he could hear that his voice was thick with disappointment.

"Then the feather was not what the rhyme meant at all," said Seaborn. He shook his head. "I am sorry," he said. "I was sure it was."

"I, too," Doss put in. He met Rowan's eyes briefly, saw the unfriendliness there, and looked down again.

"I do not agree," said Asha firmly. "I never did see how a simple feather could add anything to the brew. Feathers are used for decoration, and sometimes as a pen for writing. That is all they are ever used for."

Rowan rolled the pointed end of the feather between his fingers. Despite what Asha said, he was sure that Orin's rhyme *had* meant the feather of the green bird. Again he repeated the instructions to himself. Had he done exactly what they said?

Stir slowly with new fighter's quill,
Three times, no more, and let it still.

He had stirred the mixture with the feather. He had stirred three times, no more. He had let it still. There was nothing more. Nothing …

And then he saw it. The one word he had not considered.

He sighed. At last he knew what he had to do.

16 – The Fighter

New. That was the word that counted.

"A feather *could* add something to the brew," Rowan said to Asha. "It could add a trace of the oil it draws from the bird's body to make it waterproof. But only if it is freshly plucked. The oil must dry up and vanish into the air very quickly."

The Candidates looked up, as one, to the dimming sky above the cliff-top, where the bird shrieked and plunged, flapping and clawing at another invader. As they watched, a feather fell from the bird's wing and drifted down towards the sea far below.

"It is when the birds fight that the feathers fall," said Doss.

"We cannot climb that cliff, Doss of Pandellis," scoffed Asha. "Maris hands are not made for climbing. And the Chooser cannot go alone into such danger."

"I would be a fool to try," Rowan said unwillingly. "I am not strong enough for the climb. My arms are injured. Besides, I have no head for heights, and would probably fall."

None of the Candidates seemed to find this surprising. Of course they wouldn't, Rowan realised. Unlike Perlain, who had been surprised at how different he was from the

Rin people who came to Maris on market visits, they knew all about him. Their trainers would have told them that he was unlike most of his people, who were strong and brave by nature.

He felt his cheeks redden. Sometimes it was still hard to face this difference. Not for the first time, he wished with all his heart that Strong Jonn was with him. Jonn would not have stood here talking and being afraid. Jonn would have been half way to the cliff by now.

"The birds fight over the sea," Doss said. "The feathers fall into the water. I do not believe it would be possible to catch one from the cliff-top, even if we could reach it."

"So?" Seaborn waited impatiently. "What then are you suggesting?"

Doss looked at him, unblinking. "We wait for the bird to come to us. It will be here soon enough, when it wants more fish."

Asha nodded. "Yes. And then we trap it," she said fiercely. "And take the feather by force."

Rowan half smiled. "And with what do we trap it?" he asked.

"With our nets, of course," she answered. "What else should—? Oh!" Her mouth closed into a rigid line as she realised the problem.

Seaborn laughed. "Sadly, we have not one net between us. Thanks to your experiment in fishing, Asha!"

She turned away, furious, feeling she had been tricked.

Seaborn nodded to Rowan. "It is simple. We wait till the bird comes to the pool. But this time, we do not run from it. We face it. Make it fight us."

Rowan's heart swelled with gratitude. If Jonn could

not be with him, at least Seaborn was.

Asha spun back to face them. "Are you mad, Seaborn of Fisk?" she spat. "Have you started to *believe* yourself to be the part your trainers have taught you to play? The fearless hero, so beloved of the farmers of Rin?"

Again, Rowan felt a jolt.

Seaborn is not Jonn, he reminded himself. Seaborn is a Maris. The Maris value cunning, not strength. He must be playing a part, just as Asha says.

But Seaborn was staring Asha down. "It is you who are mad, Asha of Umbray," he said coldly. "I am what I am. And if a feather freshly plucked from the bird is what we need, I am willing to fight for it."

"One of your hands is already useless," she retorted.

Seaborn drew his knife. "Then I will use the other," he said.

"The bird is coming," warned Doss.

Trying to ignore the aching pain in his bandaged arms, Rowan picked up a stick and ran to the pool. Seaborn went with him, his knife held in his good hand. After a moment's hesitation, Doss drew out his blade and followed. But Asha gathered her silver cape around her and turned her back again.

The bird hurtled towards them. They could hear the beating of its wings. Rowan, Seaborn and Doss stood waiting, shoulder to shoulder.

It is huge, thought Rowan. Its claws are like knives. He braced himself.

"Leave the fight to us, Rowan," shouted Seaborn. "You try for the feather while we—"

His voice was drowned out by the angry screeching of

the bird. It was upon them! Rowan saw the wicked gleam of its black eyes. He staggered back as its giant wings beat the air above his head.

And then, dazed, he realised that the bird had swooped past him, past them all. It was heading straight for Asha, who was still standing stubbornly with her back to them.

"Asha!" he screamed.

She half turned, saw what was happening, and flung herself to the rocky ground. The bird skimmed over her, its beak snapping, then swooped away into the sky.

Rowan ran to her. Already she was crawling to her feet, bruised, scratched and shuddering with shock. "What happened? Why did it do that?" she gasped.

"It took no notice of us at all!" shouted Seaborn, as he and Doss ran to join them. "Yet we were at its feeding pool."

"It attacked Asha once before, and ignored the rest of us," muttered Rowan.

"But why? Why?" Asha glanced up fearfully. She raised her hand to her mouth. "It is turning!" she hissed. "It is coming for me again!"

Rowan looked up. Sure enough, high in the sky, the green bird was wheeling in a circle, preparing to attack once more.

"Hide in the forest," said Rowan urgently. "We will try to stop it."

Asha began to limp down the rock towards the trees. Her silver cloak flared and billowed behind her. Over its shining surface moved a wavering confusion of pictures: the rock, the sky, the small shape of the approaching bird, the larger shapes of Rowan, Doss and Seaborn.

Rowan's eyes widened.

"Asha!" he screamed. "Your cloak! Take it off! Take it off!"

The woman hesitated.

But Rowan was already running towards her, calling back over his shoulder for the others.

"Don't you see? Your cloak is a mirror!" Rowan gabbled as he reached Asha's side. He began tearing at the strings that held the silver cloak around her shoulders. "When you turn your back the creature sees its own reflection. So it attacks. It thinks it is fighting another of its kind."

Now Asha could not get the cloak off fast enough. It dropped to the ground, and she backed away.

Just in time. The bird had almost reached them.

"Do not waste the chance," shouted Doss, darting for the cloak and picking up one side of it. "Asha, stand back! Seaborn—hold it up with me."

Seaborn did as he was told, asking no questions. They stretched the cloak out between them. The giant bird shrieked a furious warning. Its reflection on the cloak grew larger and larger, filling the silver surface with moving, wavering green.

The bird stretched out its claws and flapped its wings in a frenzied display of anger. A rival had dared to invade its territory! It was like the one who sometimes appeared in the silver pool. But this rival was bigger. It was flapping its own wings, and stretching out its claws. It was refusing to fly away. Refusing to surrender!

Screeching, the bird beat at the cloak with its huge wings, ripped it with razor-sharp claws. Doss and Seaborn lurched and staggered, trying to keep their grip.

Again the bird threw itself at its imagined enemy. Rowan's heart leaped as a feather fell, gleaming, to the ground.

"Drop the cloak!" he screamed. "Throw it away!"

Doss and Seaborn hurled the cloak aside. It fell in a tangled, tattered heap on the rock. The bird swooped on it, tearing at it with its beak and crying out its triumph.

Rowan dived for the feather, tears springing into his eyes as pain shot through his injured arms. He pulled the precious crystal jar from his pocket. Trying to stop his fingers from shaking, he unscrewed the lid.

Stir slowly with new fighter's quill
Three times, no more, and let it still ...

The feather was still warm in his hand. The smooth, pointed end gleamed with oil. Rowan plunged it into the blue mixture. Holding his breath, he stirred slowly. Once, twice, three times.

He set the mixture on the rock in front of him and closed his eyes. He could not bear to look.

Then he heard three voices crying out. His eyes flew open.

The liquid in the jar was shining brilliant green. Green as the trees. Green as the feathers of the fighter bird. Green as the grass in the valley of Rin.

17 – The Greatest Fear

Now it was Asha's turn to be bandaged. Her hands had been grazed on the rock, her back and shoulders scratched and beaten by the bird's wings and claws.

She would not let anyone touch her wounds except Rowan. She sat rigidly as he smeared on the ointment through the tears in her clothing. It must have hurt her, but she gave not a single whimper of pain.

Doss and Seaborn stood watching from a distance. Seaborn kept looking at the sky. Finally he spoke.

"We must move quickly to find the last ingredient," he said. "Already it is dark. Night is upon us."

Rowan knew Seaborn was thinking of the Keeper's failing strength. But all Rowan could think of was his mother. How much time did she have left?

"The Choosing should be completed by now," muttered Asha. "By now the Chooser should be naming the Choice."

"How can the Keeper be so sure she will die at sunrise?" Rowan asked.

"So it has always been," said Asha. "It is part of the mystery of the Crystal. This night, of all in the year, is always the night of the Choosing. The night of the full moon. Orin found the Crystal in this month, on the night of the full moon. But always, before, the flame above the Cavern of the Crystal has been lit by sunset."

She looked at Rowan accusingly.

"It is not my fault that time is so short," Rowan exclaimed. "We came from Rin as soon as we were summoned. And I did not ask for my mother to be struck down."

The last lines of Orin's verse were ringing in his mind.

Add venom from your greatest fear—
One drop—and then the truth is clear.

What was his greatest fear? It was that he would fail to do all he had to do. That his mother would die. That a new Keeper would not be chosen in time to keep the Crystal alive. That, because of him, his land would be threatened by a last and terrible Zebak invasion. That he and Jonn, Annad, and all their friends would be taken back into slavery, and their beautiful valley destroyed.

And yet this could not be what Orin's rhyme had meant. Orin was talking about a different kind of fear. Orin was a Maris. His recipe was meant to be understood by Maris minds.

He looked at Doss, Seaborn and Asha, one by one. Pale, tense faces. Expressionless eyes.

"What is your greatest fear?" he asked.

There was only a second's hesitation. Then they all said the words together.

"The Great Serpent."

Rowan drew a deep breath. He had suspected this. But he had not wanted to think of it.

"The Great Serpent's fangs drip poison," said Doss. "I believe that is what Orin's rhyme means. We must obtain a drop of the poison, to complete the antidote."

The other two nodded.

The silence hung heavy between them. It was quiet and dark in the clearing. The fighter bird no longer shrieked at rivals on the cliff-top. And it had not returned to the pool. Perhaps it had gone to its nest for the night.

"How do we find the Great Serpent?" Rowan asked at last.

In his mind was the picture he had seen in the house of books at home in Rin. It had frightened him then. The thought of facing the real beast filled him with terror.

"The sea is full of serpents," said Seaborn. "And they are not hard to find. Venture onto the shore after the sun has gone down, and they will find you."

"But the Great Serpent?" Rowan persisted.

Asha and Seaborn glanced at Doss. And Rowan remembered what Perlain had said.

"Your eyes have the look of one who has seen the Great Serpent, and lived. Deep, and full of knowledge. Strange in a boy so young. I have known only one other."

He turned to Doss. "You have seen it," he said quietly.

Doss nodded. "I have." He did not look at Rowan as he spoke.

Rowan waited. He knew that if he waited long enough, Doss would speak again.

"It was at exactly this time, a year ago," Doss murmured finally. "That day I was with my family, in our boat. There was to be a full moon that night, as there would be at the Choosing. It was my Day of Farewell."

"Each Candidate has a Day of Farewell," Seaborn said, in reply to Rowan's enquiring look. "It is the day we say goodbye to our families. After that we live apart from the rest of Maris. We retire to our clan's Candidate house, with only our trainers and our books for company, to prepare in earnest for the Choosing."

"That must be hard," said Rowan, thinking how he would feel to be separated from everyone and everything he knew and loved.

"It is necessary," said Seaborn.

"And it is preparation, too," Asha added. "For a new Keeper is taken to the surface and shown to the people only once. After that he or she returns to the Cavern of the Crystal, for ever."

Rowan felt a cold thrill of horror.

"You mean—Keepers never again leave the Cavern?" he stammered. "Never see their homes and friends, or breathe the open air, or see the sky?"

Doss smiled. "They do not need to do so, Rowan. The Crystal is all to them."

"They are there to serve," said Seaborn.

Rowan closed his eyes. To him, this sounded like a living death. Now he realised what Perlain had meant when he said that to be Keeper was not a thing everyone desired.

"You do not understand," Doss said. "It is not pain, but joy."

"It is a glorious duty," said Asha. "So it has always been." Her eyes glowed.

Rowan told himself that this was not his business. It was not for him to judge the ways of the Maris.

"Tell me about the Great Serpent, Doss," he said abruptly.

"We had sailed far," said Doss. "We were thinking of turning for home, when our boat began to take in water. Not just from one place, but from many. The wood had been pierced, and then the holes had been filled cleverly with something that fell away only after a long time, when the boat was out of sight of land."

He was staring straight ahead. He accused no one. But Seaborn and Asha frowned.

"My clan did not touch your boat!" snapped Asha.

"Nor mine," said Seaborn.

Still Doss did not look at them. "However it happened, the boat sank," he said. "We swam, but the tide was strong." He was speaking so softly that Rowan had to lean forward to hear him.

"Soon I lost sight of my mother and father, and my brothers," the quiet voice went on. "I fought the tide. I was exhausted. The sun began to set. And then I heard a sound. A high, ringing sound. It seemed to come from all around me. From the sky above, and the sea beneath. It grew louder. It went on and on. It filled my ears, and seemed to enter my brain and fill it too, so that I could think of nothing else. It was the singing of the Great Serpent."

Again the picture that Rowan had seen rose up in his mind. The boat, and the people screaming, with their hands over their ears. He shuddered.

Doss's voice had become flat and lifeless, a chant, as if he were reciting a lesson repeated many times. "The Great Serpent came up from the depths. It towered above me. Its

111

eyes were golden, and full of ancient secrets. Its scales glittered like fire in the setting sun. It looked at me. I knew that I was going to die."

"But you didn't," Rowan breathed. His own heart was beating rapidly. He knew what it was to face nightmares.

"No," Doss said simply. "Blackness closed in on me. I know nothing of what happened after that. I remember nothing of the night. But when I awoke, the sun was rising, and I was lying on part of my family's boat, drifting in sight of the shore. My clan saw me, and brought me in. They searched for the others, too. But no one was ever found."

He turned his dreamy eyes on Rowan. "I alone of my family was spared. And I—was changed. I could feel it. Everyone around me could see it. It was as though something had been lost—or added. I do not know which."

"It is a wonder," said Asha harshly, "that your clan allowed you to remain their Candidate. Were there not others, undamaged, who could have taken your place?"

"Of course," Doss replied. "And I expected this. But then I realised that my trainers believed the change was for the good. It had not affected my wits. But it separated me from others. Made me different. And, they thought, special."

Again, a strange smile hovered on his lips. "For, of course, to see the Great Serpent, and live, is a powerful charm. No one is known to have done it since Orin the Wise."

Seaborn, who had been listening in silence, finally spoke. "There are some who say the whole story is a lie," he growled. "A lie invented by your trainers, to impress the people, and, one day, the Chooser. As perhaps it is doing at this moment."

Doss met his cold gaze calmly. "I wish it was a lie," he said. "For then that sound, and those yellow eyes, would not haunt my dreams ... as after this night they may haunt yours."

... as after this night they may haunt yours.

Rowan straightened his shoulders. Whatever his fears, whatever his doubts, he knew that the only way for him to go was forward.

"The sun has set," he said. "Time is short. And we must find the Great Serpent. How do you think we should begin?"

18 – The Moon of the Choosing

I do not see how it is possible," said Asha. "Only fools venture on to the deep by night, even in a boat. And we have no boat. If we swim, we will surely be taken by the smaller serpents without ever sighting the great one we seek."

The sky was dark, and filled with stars. The moon-flower showed white in the dark pool. Waves crashed on the shore beyond the forest.

"There must be a way," said Rowan, watching Doss. "Because Orin did it. The answer lies with him."

To see the Great Serpent, and live, is a powerful charm. No one is known to have done it since Orin the Wise.

Orin the Wise ...

A thousand years ago, on the day he found the Crystal, Orin met the Great Serpent, thought Rowan. It was just at this time of year. That is why this is always the time of the Choosing.

He went over the story in his mind. The story Perlain had told him. Orin was fishing. He started for home in his boat, after sunset. The Great Serpent rose from the sea. It upset his boat, and chased him. He fled to the Island. He found the Crystal.

And that is how all this began, Rowan thought. Then he frowned.

There was something odd about the story. Some detail that was wrong. At first Rowan could not think what it was. And then he remembered.

Orin had not been fishing on the day he found the Crystal. The Keeper had let slip that Orin was actually on the Island that day, making the antidote for Death Sleep.

Rowan thought it through. Orin must have just said he was fishing, to hide his real purpose. He did not want others to know he was making the secret Death Sleep antidote. And no one then, or since, had questioned his story.

No one had questioned it because Orin had brought the Crystal back with him, and all interest was focused on its wonder. And after that, no one questioned the story because Orin had become Orin the Wise. Someone extraordinary. The first Keeper of the Crystal.

But on the day Orin found the Crystal he was still just an ordinary Maris man. And when you thought about it like that, the story of his meeting with the Great Serpent was even more unlikely.

Would Orin's fear of staying on the Island overnight have been greater than his fear of taking a boat into dark water? Almost certainly not.

And even if he had braved the water, could Orin really have out-swum the Great Serpent if it was chasing him? Again, almost certainly not.

Rowan's thoughts ran on.

That part of the story too, then, was a lie. Orin had not left the Island after sunset. He had not met the beast in the sea.

Had he really seen it at all?

Yes, because its poison was the fourth ingredient in the antidote.

So ... The back of Rowan's neck prickled. So that meant something very strange indeed. It meant that somehow Orin and the Great Serpent had met on land. On the Island. Perhaps even ...

"Look at the moon," murmured Doss, pointing.

A great full moon had risen over the treetops. Still, cold and white, it floated in the grey sky like the flower in the depths of the dark pool.

"The Moon of the Choosing," whispered Asha.

And then they heard it. A heavy, slithering sound, coming from the path through the forest. Coming closer.

"What is it?" panted Seaborn.

Doss stood, his eyes wide. "Quickly," he hissed. "Away from here! Away!"

They ran from the rock, and crouched among the trees.

The sound grew louder. The sound of leaves being crushed and swept aside. The sound of ferns being bent and broken under a giant weight.

Into the clearing writhed the Great Serpent, leaving behind it a cleared path, as it had done so many times before. The water of the deep still dripped from its dragon head. Its yellow eyes were glazed. Its drying golden scales shone under the Moon of the Choosing. Its huge, swollen body thrashed and curled.

Waves of terror flowed over Rowan. He heard the soft whimpering of Doss, the heavy breathing of Asha and Seaborn, close beside him. He slipped his hand into his pocket and gripped the small, hard jar, the jar that contained the mixture that would save his mother's life. If one small thing was added. One drop ...

"Why is it here?" whispered Asha, in dread. "Why does it invade the land? The deep—the deep is the Great Serpent's kingdom. So it has always been."

But Rowan had guessed. "Once a year it comes here," he whispered back. *This* is how it has always been. But you did not know it, for it happens on this side of the Island. The side you in Maris never see, once the sun has set."

The scent of the moon-flower was strong in the air. It billowed from the pool. The serpent writhed towards it, slowly, painfully climbing the rock.

"It is looking for us," hissed Seaborn, in an agony of fear.

"No," Rowan said. "It does not even know we are here. There is something else it seeks. A place. Watch. Wait."

The serpent reached the pool at the top of the rock. It stared with its yellow eyes at the moon-flower, floating white in the rippling water. Then it looked up at the moon in the sky. It opened its massive jaws, and cried out. A weird, ringing sound that pierced the ears, and filled the mind.

Doss wrapped his arms around his head and moaned softly.

Asha, too, hid her eyes.

But Seaborn watched, fascinated, as the monster coiled its enormous body around the pool.

"It is laying eggs," he breathed.

"Yes," said Rowan. "It is like the giant turtles that swim in your seas. Like the Kirrian Worm, whose eggs you collect every spring morning. It lives in the deep, but it lays its eggs on land. And this is its place. This is where Orin found it."

The serpent was laying eggs indeed. They shone silver in the moonlight. As each was laid, the tip of the great tail swept it into the moon-flower pool, where it sank through the water to rest on the bed of silver sand.

"What better place to hide the eggs." Rowan was filled with wonder. "No creature could dare to touch them there. The shells must be hard as stone, so that the fish cannot harm them."

By now, Doss and Asha were looking too. "But when they hatch—" Asha began.

"By the time they hatch, the fish will not be so many," Rowan said quietly. "The fighter bird will have taken a great number of them."

"The fish that are left will attack the new-born serpents," nodded Doss. "And many will be killed. But some will survive, swimming to the surface, crawling out of the pool, wriggling down the path to the shore, and into the sea."

"And the broken shells will remain, gradually to be ground down by the moving water to make more of the silver sand," said Seaborn. "By Orin, it is incredible." His face was alive with interest. He was so entranced that he had forgotten his fear.

"If it were not for the fighter bird, the pool would be thick with fish, and the baby serpents would all die when they hatched," Rowan whispered. "If the fighter bird did not defend the pool against all its neighbours, the pool would be emptied of every last fish. Then all the eggs would hatch safely, and the sea would be thick with serpents, but empty of every other living thing."

"No fish," said Doss. "No food for Maris, oil for our lamps, fish skin for our shoes and clothing. No safety, even in daylight, for the ships that come to trade, because the serpents would be hungry, and desperate. And so the Maris would die. And the serpents, too, in the end. It is all a great whole."

"It is meaningless!" Seaborn was scowling now. "The birds eat the fish. The fish eat the serpents. Why need the cycle exist at all? If we were to come to the Island each year and destroy the Great Serpent's eggs, using the way Rowan has taught us, our seas would soon be completely free of danger. We could fish at night as well as by day, and so double our catch, or triple it. We could sell to the traders, and feed multitudes."

"The Island is forbidden by Orin, Seaborn of Fisk," said Asha sternly. "And the serpents have always existed in our seas. That is the way it has always been."

For Asha, that was enough.

But not for Seaborn.

"Why should we not destroy the serpents?" he demanded. "Of what use are they? All they do is stop us fishing when we wish."

Do you not see it, Seaborn? Rowan thought. Do you not see the use? You yourself have just explained it.

But he said nothing. Instead, he stood up. He was trembling all over, but he knew what he had to do. He unscrewed the lid of the silver-topped jar, and stepped towards the rock.

19 – One Drop

he Great Serpent turned its head. Its yellow eyes were fixed on Rowan.

"Do not look at it," Doss cried.

But it was too late. Already Rowan was staring into those glazed eyes. And he couldn't look away. It was as though his body had gone numb.

Hands tugged at his sleeve. "Rowan!" came a choking voice. "Remember! Your mother! The poison!"

Rowan tore his eyes away from that cold, golden stare. Doss, Asha and Seaborn were behind him. Their faces shone ghastly white in the moonlight.

It was Asha who had spoken. Dimly Rowan realised that she had at last used his name. She grabbed his arm fiercely.

"You are the Chooser. You must not do this. I will go in your place. My death would be of no account. Yours will mean the end of Maris. Give me the jar."

He looked into her pale eyes. They were full of fear, but met his own steadily. She *is* like my mother, he thought. She will always do what she feels is right. Even to her death.

Seaborn shook his head. "I am stronger, and taller," he

said in a low voice. "It is for me to face the beast. Give me the jar."

On the rock, the serpent waited.

Rowan hesitated, then turned to Doss, a small blue shadow in the dim light.

"No," Doss said quietly. "None of us can do this thing in Rowan's place."

Asha and Seaborn broke out in angry argument, but Doss held up his hand.

"From birth we have feared this creature and its kind. And it knows us, and our kind. It knows our smell. It knows our pale skin. It knows how we move. We are its natural prey. It will strike out at us without thinking. The only one of us with any chance of creeping close to it is the one who is the stranger."

Rowan took a deep breath. "Yes," he said.

He turned back and faced the beast again. This time he did not meet its eyes. He took a step forward. And another.

The serpent did not move, but its huge jaws opened, a black, forked tongue flickered out, and it hissed. The inside of its mouth was smooth and yellow. Its fangs were white, tipped with black. Poison dripped from the black needlepoints like drops of steaming liquid gold and fell, sizzling, to the ground.

Rowan climbed. He could feel the rock smooth under his feet. He could hear himself panting. He clutched the jar tightly.

His foot brushed against something on the ground. It was the dead moon-flower. Already brown and dried-out, its petals were curled like shallow cups of leather. He knelt, and tore one away.

The serpent was still laying eggs. Still pushing them one by one into the pool. The moon above it shone huge and white. But its yellow eyes were fixed on Rowan.

Doss was right, Rowan thought. It does not quite know what I am. And it wants to finish laying its eggs. It will threaten, but it will not stir unless I make a sudden movement. There is a chance.

He crept up towards the pool. Nearer, nearer … till he could see the moon-flower shining beneath the dark water, like a reflection of the moon above. He began to edge around the vast coils that encircled the pool, moving towards the head.

The Great Serpent's eyes blazed. It arched its neck, and its eerie, ringing cry split the air.

The sound was so piercing that tears sprang into Rowan's eyes. He longed to cover his ears. But he had the flower petal in one hand, and the precious jar in the other. He could do nothing.

And then the serpent hissed again. Its jaws, which could crush a Maris boat to splinters, gaped wide. Its tongue flickered, tasting the air. Its fangs glinted in the moonlight, white tipped with black, dripping deadly liquid gold.

Now! Rowan darted forward, holding out the moon-flower petal, catching the venom in the leathery dish it had become.

The serpent struck at him, screaming its anger. Rowan lurched backwards and fell, the sound tearing into his brain. Pain shot through his bandaged arms. The venom smoked and sizzled in the moon-flower petal. The jar tilted dangerously.

Add venom from your greatest fear—
One drop—

In panic, Rowan looked at the jar. The green liquid was still safe. Then he turned his eyes to the petal, and to his horror saw that the venom was burning through it. The precious golden liquid was trickling away through black, scorched holes, and falling to waste on the rock. It was falling in a fine, smoking stream. Almost gone.

"No!" He was hardly aware that he had screamed.

"Rowan, get away! Oh—oh, in the name of Orin, run! Run! It is stirring! It is going to—"

The shrieking of the three Maris sounded dimly in his ears. He was aware of a monstrous shape rising above him, blocking out the moon. Of great slithering coils unwinding from around the pool. Of dripping jaws opening to strike again.

But the antidote …

One drop …

With trembling hands he tipped the petal over the jar.

And one last golden drop fell, hissing, into the darkness of the shadowed green liquid. Turning it clear. Clear as the water in the pool. Clear as the glass of the jar. Clear as truth.

"Rowan!"

He clapped the silver lid on the jar. He stumbled to his feet. He leaped for his life, tumbling down the smooth brown surface of the rock, his prize clutched in his throbbing hands.

But the beast was roaring its rage, thrashing and twisting after him with terrifying speed. He could hear it behind him—close, and closer every second. Dazed with pain and terror, he plunged forward. Where should he go? Which way should he run?

"Here!"

The three Maris were calling him. Through a blur he saw them running to meet him, their own faces twisted with fear.

Blindly Rowan held out his hands. Asha and Seaborn caught hold of him and swung him down from the rock and into the trees. Half dragging him, they began to struggle away through the trackless wood.

Thickets of bush and fern choked their way on every side. Vines hung thickly from the trees, twisting and tangling, catching at their hands, feet and clothes, holding them back. Leaves formed a roof over their heads, cutting out the light of the moon. Seaborn and Asha pulled Rowan between them. Doss struggled on behind.

The monster bellowed. Trees cracked and fell as, shrieking and hissing, it writhed after them. It did not need light. It was following their sound, and their scent. Every second it drew closer. They tore their way through the undergrowth, sobbing and gasping, blind in the darkness, the terrible cries ringing in their ears. So Orin must have run, in terror for his life.

"Which way?" Rowan heard Asha wailing. "I cannot see!"

And then there was a terrified, choking yell from behind them.

At first, straining his eyes against the blackness, Rowan could not see what had happened. Then he saw. Doss was caught in a looping vine. It had twisted around his neck, and his struggles to free himself had tightened it. He was choking, and trapped.

The beast was almost upon them. They could see the trees shaking and falling in its path. It howled as it smelled their terror. Doss hung, helpless, the tips of his toes kicking uselessly at the soft ground.

"Leave him!" shrieked Asha.

But Rowan could not. He twisted from her grasp, and from Seaborn's clutching hands, and darted back to where Doss hung.

He clawed at the choking vine with his fingers, ignoring his wounds. Agonising pain shot through his bandaged arms.

Doss gave a strangled scream. Then a knife cut cleanly through the vine, and he fell to the ground. He lay there, fainting.

"Get up!" hissed Asha, kicking at him. The knife that had freed him glinted dully in her hand.

Seaborn bent and swept Doss into his arms.

"Quickly!" he gasped. And staggering with his burden he lunged away once more, with Rowan and Asha close behind him.

They blundered on through inky blackness.

"Leave me," rasped Doss, stirring. "Put me down. Leave me. The Chooser must live ... The Crystal must live ..."

"Be still. The Chooser will not leave you," panted Seaborn.

"There!" shrieked Asha. "Oh, there!"

She was pointing at a winking light. So faint, so small, it shone through the black trees like a star.

"Maris!" cried Seaborn.

They struggled on, towards the light. It grew larger and brighter. They began to hear the crashing of waves. Never could they have found their way so quickly in the daylight. But in the night the Maris lights gleamed across the water, piercing the darkness, guiding them.

Hissing, writhing, the serpent plunged behind them. The land was not its place. But it was angry. It was hungry. It was hunting.

Struggling for breath, crying with fear, they burst out of the forest and onto the shore. Huge waves beat upon the rocks. Salt spray tingled on their faces. Across the water, every house in Maris blazed with light.

"They have lit every lamp for us," gasped Seaborn, letting Doss slip to the ground at last. "They must—they must all be—waiting."

"Hurry!" urged Asha.

There, in front of them, was the iron gate.

Dragging Doss between them, they ran to it and wrenched it open. Together they tumbled into the darkness of the stairs, and just as the great beast tore its way through the last ring of trees, the gate clanged shut behind them.

They heard the creature's tail thrashing in fury. They saw its huge head darting this way and that as it looked for them.

They clung together, trembling and exhausted. But they knew they were safe. The beast could not follow them into this small space. Like Orin before them, they had escaped.

Rowan touched the jar in his pocket. And like Orin, he thought, we are bringing back something precious.

Precious, if it was not too late.

His shaking voice echoed against the rock walls of the tunnel. "Come," he said. "We must hurry."

20 – The Deceiver

They half limped, half ran through the tunnel. It seemed endless. Ahead was only darkness.

"Where is the light of the Crystal?" panted Asha. "We must be nearly at the Cavern, and yet I cannot see it. What if ..."

"The Keeper is alive," said Seaborn firmly. "Or the people would not have been in their houses, burning lights for us."

"There!" called Rowan.

He pointed at a dim glow just colouring the blackness ahead.

They hurried towards it. Rowan's head was pounding in time with his heart. His throat felt closed and tight.

They were nearly at the Cavern, and yet he felt nothing. No unseen pull of the Crystal, drawing him. No voice whispering in his mind like his own thoughts.

They were at the entrance. Within, all was silent except for the ceaseless dripping of water. Seaborn, Doss and Asha fell back. Rowan took a breath, and crept in, afraid of what he might find.

The Keeper was huddled in her chair in the centre of the Cavern. The Crystal glowed feebly under her hands, spreading a circle of green light around her chair, and leaving the rest of the room in dimness.

In the shadows Jonn knelt by Jiller's couch, his head bowed. Rowan's heart gave a great thud.

"So, Chooser of Rin. You have returned."

The Keeper had not moved, or looked up. But her low voice filled the room.

Jonn's head jerked up. He leaped to his feet. And by the look of wild, unbelieving hope on his face Rowan knew that, after all, he was not too late.

He ran across the room and knelt down beside his mother. Yes. She still breathed. But faintly. So faintly.

His teeth were chattering. He was shaking all over. His fingers were stiff and clumsy as he pulled the jar from his pocket, and unscrewed the lid.

"I have the antidote, Keeper," he said, looking back over his shoulder. "How much should I use?"

Still the Keeper did not move. But he thought he saw her thin mouth curve into a smile.

"It seems you are everything they say, Rowan of Rin," she said. "Dip your finger into the brew, just once, and smear it on her lips. That will be enough."

The liquid in the jar was cold. It tingled on his finger as he rubbed it onto his mother's mouth.

Jiller frowned slightly in her sleep. Then, sighing, she licked her lips.

Jonn's strong hand gripped Rowan's shoulder.

"When—?" Rowan began.

"Soon." The Keeper's voice was dry and hushed, like the rustling of dead leaves. "Death Sleep takes two full hours to show itself. You cannot expect it to be undone in moments. But we cannot wait. I cannot wait. The Crystal dims. My time comes soon. Very soon. Step into the light."

"The Choosing ..." Rowan began, staggering to his feet.

The Keeper looked up. Behind her stood Doss, Seaborn and Asha, but she paid no attention to them. Her huge, pale eyes, dimming like the Crystal, sought Rowan in the darkness.

"Step into the light, Chooser of Rin," she repeated.

Rowan did as she asked.

She gazed into his face. "The flame is alight. The Choosing is completed," she said.

Rowan's mouth fell open. He glanced up and past the Keeper to the silent figures of the Candidates. Their eyes were wide with shock and disbelief.

"Keeper, the Choosing has not yet begun," he stammered. "The tests—"

"The trials you have just completed *were* the tests," she said.

Rowan stared at her.

Wearily she closed her eyes. "The old tests are no longer of use. More and more, the Candidates study for them. And study the people of Rin, too, so they may win their Chooser's favour. They are locked away from their fellows. From life itself. This is no way to choose a Maris leader. Long ago, I realised it was a mistake. I realised it when I saw that I myself could never do more than guard the Crystal. That I could not lead the Maris, or change their ways."

"You—" Rowan caught his breath. He looked wildly back at the watchful Jonn, at Jiller, lying still and silent on the couch.

He swung back to face the Keeper. Understanding

flooded through him on a red tide of anger that washed away fear and doubt.

"It was you!" he hissed. "*You* planned all this. *You* gave my mother Death Sleep."

"You dare to accuse *me* ..." The voice was low, and full of warning. But Rowan cared nothing for that.

"Yes, I accuse you," he shouted. "You just admitted that the poison took two full hours to work. That means Mother took the poison when she first came to this Cavern. Before she even met the Candidates. Before she set foot on the Island."

He pointed at the Keeper with one bandaged hand. "You did it. You planned it all. You tricked me, and the Candidates, and you risked my mother's life! Just because you wanted to set tests for which no one was prepared!"

The Keeper opened her eyes, and for a moment the Crystal glowed with its old green fire.

"The Choosing must reveal the truth," she said. "The Crystal provides the knowledge, the experience, and the power. But the Keeper provides the care and cunning. The Keeper must be able to solve new problems, as well as old ones. The Keeper must be able to change as the sea changes, dare to try ways that have not been tried. Only then will Maris survive."

"You nearly killed my mother," Rowan panted.

"The death of one is of no account."

"And you risked so much else."

"Not so much, perhaps. For I trusted the Crystal, as I always have, and it told me all would be well. That you would succeed, and return in time. I had to break the chains that bind us. I did it in the only way I could. I used you.

131

The one person I knew was not like the others of Rin."

They have collected news of you since the day you were born ...

Rowan stared at her. He should have realised that if the Candidates knew him, so did the Keeper. She, more than any.

"The Choosing is completed," droned the Keeper. "Name your Choice."

Rowan raised his eyes to the three Candidates standing behind the Keeper's chair.

Asha. Seaborn. Doss. He had grown to admire all of them. They had all stood by him when he faced the Great Serpent. And he knew now that none of them had been playing a part.

Seaborn really was brave and strong, and loved life, like Jonn. He had been chosen as Candidate by the clan of Fisk because of that. He was unusual for a Maris, but they thought he would please the Chooser of Rin.

Asha really was dutiful, honest and plain-speaking, like Jiller. She had been chosen by the clan of Umbray because of that. She was unusual for a Maris, but they thought she would please the Chooser of Rin.

And Doss. Doss really was dreamy. He cared for living things, and he had faced death, like Rowan himself. He had been chosen by the clan of Pandellis because of that. He was unusual for a Maris, but they thought he would please the Chooser of Rin.

All three Candidates had helped Rowan to solve the riddle of the antidote to Death Sleep. Each in their own way. But which one had shown the most care and cunning, the willingness to try new ways, that the Keeper had said the Maris needed?

"Name your Choice," said the Keeper weakly. "You—must—name it. Speak!"

The Crystal flickered.

Hurrying footsteps sounded on the stairs. Through the veil of water burst Perlain.

"Sails. We have seen sails," he gasped. "The horizon is filled with them. And they are moving in. It is the Zebak!"

21 – The Choice

Why do they come now?" Asha cried. "It is sense-less! They can surely see the flame of the Choosing. The time to attack would have been before, when the Crystal was weak, and the Choosing had not been completed."

"We have heard they have grown cunning. Perhaps they have a plan we know nothing about," said Seaborn grimly. "Or perhaps they hope the Crystal may yet fail before the new Keeper is joined to it."

"Rowan!" cried Perlain. "Name your Choice. The Crystal dims."

Rowan heard an exclamation behind him, and turned. Jonn was bending over Jiller. Her eyes were open. She was smiling at him.

"I have been asleep," she murmured. "And Jonn, I had such wonderful dreams." Then a slight frown creased her forehead. "But where am I? Where is Rowan?"

Pure joy filled Rowan's heart. But it lasted only an instant. His mother lived. She was awake, and happy. But the Zebak were coming. He had to act. He had to name the new Keeper and renew the Crystal's life, or they were all lost.

He turned again to the Candidates.

"The Keeper has told me to look for care, and cunning, and the willingness to try new ways," he said rapidly. "She has said that the Crystal will supply everything else."

He looked into Asha's burning eyes. "You—you are good, and you will always do what you think is right," he stammered. "But your mind is not open. You cling to the rules and the old ways, and live only by those. So while I admire you, I cannot choose you."

Her expression did not change, but she bowed her head.

Rowan turned to Seaborn. "You are brave, and strong," he said. "And you are willing to try new ways. But you often act in haste, without the care and cunning the Keeper seeks. So while I hope we will always be friends, I cannot choose you."

Seaborn, too, bowed his head. But as he did, his eyes seemed to flash with something—something almost like relief. Rowan wondered about it only for a second. There was no time now for anything except the Choice.

He moved to Doss, and put his hand on his shoulder. They looked at one another. A long, searching look.

I pray I am right, thought Rowan.

"You must say the words," Perlain reminded him softly.

Rowan swallowed. "The Chooser has made the Choice," he said. He felt Doss's shoulder stiffen suddenly under his fingers. "Let the other Candidates leave this place."

Doss stood rigidly still. His eyes were blank, as though he saw nothing.

His usually calm face tense, Perlain took Asha and Seaborn through the veil of water, and then returned.

The Crystal glowed feebly. Once, twice, three times. The Keeper stirred. "The doors are locked and will not open again until the new Keeper wills," she breathed. "Make haste. Soon the sun will rise."

"Doss of Pandellis," said Perlain quickly. "The Crystal."

Doss moved to the Keeper's chair like one in a dream. Stiffly he stretched out his hand towards the Crystal's soft glow. Rowan looked curiously at his blank, unseeing eyes.

The eyes of one who has seen the Great Serpent, and lived.

It is right, Rowan told himself. My Choice is right. Doss has everything the Keeper asked for. And he was meant for this task. Like Orin, he saw the Great Serpent. And after that, he was changed.

Yet there was something wrong. Rowan could feel it.

Doss's hand hovered over the Crystal.

"Join with the Crystal, and with me," murmured the Keeper.

I saw the Great Serpent, too, Rowan thought suddenly. And so did Asha and Seaborn. But we are not changed. Why then was Doss? What happened to him, a year ago?

I remember nothing of the night ... I was changed ... Something was lost—or added. I do not know which.

What had happened to Doss during that long night, under the full moon, out of sight of land?

Under the full moon ...

"Wait!" Rowan burst out. He grabbed Doss's hand. His voice echoed, shockingly loud, around the Cavern. Jonn and Jiller looked up, startled, and Perlain gripped the back of the Keeper's chair.

Slowly Doss turned. He stared blankly, first at Rowan, then at the hand that gripped his own.

"Doss, you could not have seen the Great Serpent a year ago," gabbled Rowan.

"Rowan, this does not matter now," shouted Perlain. "For Orin's sake, do you not see? The Keeper is dying. Letting go of her life. The ceremony has begun. It must continue. The Zebak ..."

Doss's mouth opened. "The Chooser has made the Choice," he said flatly. "Let the other Candidates depart this place."

Rowan was shivering, but still he held fast to the cold, webbed hand. "In this month, at the full moon, the Great Serpent is on the Island laying its eggs. We know that now. Doss, you could not have seen it far out to sea."

"Rowan!" cried Jiller. "Let him go!"

Jonn sprang up and in two strides was by Rowan's side. "Rowan, let his hand go," he whispered urgently. "Nothing matters now. All questions can be answered later."

But Rowan knew the questions couldn't wait.

"Doss, speak to me!" he begged. "What is wrong with you? Tell me what happened to you that night. What changed you? It was not the Great Serpent. What was it?"

"The Great Serpent came up from the depths," droned Doss. "It towered above me. Its eyes were golden, and full of ancient secrets."

Rowan listened in horror. Doss was using the same words exactly as the ones he had used on the Island. Even his voice was the same. He was chanting, as though repeating a lesson learned by heart.

And he believes it, thought Rowan. He believes it. But it is not true!

"Its scales glittered like fire in the setting sun," chanted Doss. "It looked at me. I knew that I was going to die."

"This is not something you have seen in truth!" Rowan

exclaimed. "This is something put into your mind by someone else!"

A terrible fear seized him. "Doss, who arranged for your boat to be damaged?" he cried. "Who was waiting for you out there, beyond the horizon? Who picked you up from the dark sea and kept you all night, then sent you back with only a false memory of what had happened to you?"

But he knew the answer. And by the terrified look on Perlain's face, he could see that the Maris man knew, too. There was only one possible explanation.

They have grown cunning ...

"A Zebak boat picked you up!" he breathed. "By some means, the Zebak bent you to their will that night, Doss. They buried secret orders deep within your mind, and covered them with the false memory of the Great Serpent. When you came back to Maris, people saw you were changed, but they did not know the real reason. And why should they? Because even you did not."

"It is impossible," Rowan heard Jonn muttering to Jiller. "The boy's trainers would have seen it. The Keeper would have seen it."

"No!" Rowan exclaimed, without looking around. "A year ago, the Keeper's power had already dimmed. And no one else could have seen it, because part of the plan must have been that the secret orders would only come to the surface of Doss's mind when certain words were said."

He looked straight into Doss's blank eyes. "I said those words just a few moments ago, didn't I? They are always said when a Keeper is chosen. 'The Chooser has made the Choice.'"

Doss quivered, staring.

Rowan's stomach churned. It was horrible to see the familiar face so changed. "I saw and felt it happen, Doss. I wondered what was wrong then, and now I know. At that moment, you lost your own will. You became the servant of the Zebak. That is why their ships have come now. They saw the flame, and knew their time had come. They are waiting for your signal that the Crystal, and this land, are theirs."

Perlain groaned. He had covered his face with his hands and was rocking slowly backwards and forwards.

"Perlain!" said Rowan sharply. "Do not waste time despairing! Bring Seaborn and Asha back!"

Perlain shook his head.

"Quickly!" shouted Rowan. "Do you not understand? Doss cannot be Keeper. He will betray Maris. He will betray us all!"

"Look out!" shrieked Jiller.

Before all of them, she had seen the knife flashing in Doss's free hand.

With a cry, Jonn leaped forward and gripped the knife as it plunged towards the dying Keeper's heart. He wrestled Doss aside, and held him. Doss struggled wildly for a moment, then suddenly gave in. He hung in Jonn's grip, limp and still.

"The Chooser has made the Choice," he mumbled. "If the Choice is not Doss of Pandellis, the Keeper must die. The Crystal must die."

"Perlain!" Rowan screamed. "Why are you waiting? Bring—"

"The doors are locked," said Perlain. His voice was filled with despair. "They will open for none but the

Keeper. And the Keeper cannot be roused. She is beyond our reach."

"Then you!" said Jonn roughly. "You, Perlain. You must join with the Crystal yourself. It may not be what you would wish. But better you as Keeper than none."

Perlain shook his head again. "I cannot," he said. "I am not known by the Crystal. If I touch it, I will die."

"Then what are we going to do?" Rowan cried out in desperation. "Perlain, what are we going to do?"

Perlain looked at him. "There is only one thing we can do," he said. "Apart from Doss of Pandellis, there is only one person here now who can touch the Crystal and live. Only one person who can join with it, to become Keeper of Maris. And that is you."

22 – Terror

N o!" The word burst from Rowan's lips and echoed around the Cavern. He backed away from the Keeper's chair, the dying Crystal, shaking his head over and over again.

Never to see home again. Never to see the sky, the green hills, the stream, the snow on the Mountain. Never to feel the fresh, sweet air on his face, or hear the sounds of birds. Never. To spend the rest of his life below the earth, swallowed up, dissolved, in the great mystery of the Crystal.

"No," he repeated. "No!"

"You must do it," said Perlain.

"I am not of Maris," cried Rowan. "I cannot—"

"You can," said Perlain. "And if you do not, we are lost." He held out his hands to Jiller. "Tell him," he shouted.

Rowan spun round to face his mother. Tears were rolling down her cheeks. "You must do it. You are the only one," she whispered. "The Crystal does not know me now. Only you. Only you …"

"Quickly!" hissed Perlain. "There is no time."

Rowan turned to Jonn, who still held the silent Doss. Jonn's mouth was grim and set. His eyes were full of pain as he nodded.

There was nowhere left for Rowan to turn, except to his own heart. And he knew that he had no choice. By giving up the things he loved, he might be able to save them. By refusing to give them up, he would almost certainly destroy them.

He straightened his shoulders, and walked to the Keeper. The Crystal lay like a stone in her lap. Only a tiny spark in its heart remained, lighting her hands with its dull green glow.

Rowan put his hands on hers. She opened her eyes.

"You ..." she sighed. "Why?"

"There is no one else," said Rowan softly. Behind him he heard Jiller's low sobbing.

The Keeper closed her eyes again. She was beyond wonder, and questions. But her lips moved. Rowan bent down to hear what she was saying.

"I say the words, but no one believes. Nothing can stand against the power of the Crystal," breathed the voice in his ear. "Feel ... and ... understand."

And it was as though Rowan was falling—slowly, slowly, drifting through swirling ages of time and memory. He could no longer see the Cavern. No longer hear his mother's voice. He felt himself letting go. Giving himself up to the power, not with sadness, but with deep joy.

And as he sank deeper ... deeper, he knew that he was becoming part of something greater than himself. It was like a sea that was deep, broad, and as old as time.

Nothing could stand against it. No love of clan, of family. No ties, or claims of others. All was washing away. His very self—his loves, fears, hopes, mistakes—everything that bound him to his life was slipping from him. He struggled a little, not wanting to let them go.

Feel ... and ... understand.

Had the Keeper spoken again? Or was it a memory? The hands beneath his stirred.

Nothing can stand against the power of the Crystal ...

Then Rowan understood. At last, he understood.

Help me, Keeper, he called in his mind. *Help me to do as I must.*

He felt a surge of power. And then he was crying out aloud. He was pulling one hand from the Crystal, bending backwards, and reaching out for the still, pale figure of Doss.

"Rowan!" Dimly he heard his mother scream. But he knew what he had to do.

He gripped Doss's hand, and dragged him away from Jonn. He felt the great healing power rushing through him into Doss like a river flowing into the sea.

Then, using the last of his strength, he pulled Doss forward. He guided Doss's small webbed hands over the Keeper's hands, and took his own away.

The separation hit him like a blow. He staggered back from the chair, and fell to his knees on the ground. His chest was filled with the sudden pain of loneliness and loss. Tears blinded him.

He became aware that the Cavern was echoing with sound.

"What have you done?" Perlain was shouting in panic.

"Rowan! Rowan!" Jiller was crying.

He tried to speak, but the words choked in his throat. He crawled backwards, away from the dazzling light. The

Crystal was shining, brighter and brighter. It was alive with fire, sparkling with every colour of the earth, sea and sky. Colour and light filled the air, lit the streaming Cavern walls like rainbows ...

And then it was finished. The tiny, wizened body of the old Keeper lay like an empty shell on the chair. A new Keeper stood looking at them. His eyes were the deep, grave eyes of Doss of Pandellis. But he stood straighter and taller than Doss ever had. His clothes were no longer blue, but of no colour and all colours at once, like shining water. And in his hands the Crystal flashed and burned like a star.

Perlain fell back, and bowed. "I greet you, Keeper of the Crystal," he murmured. His face was stiff with terror.

"The sun is rising," said the Keeper. He turned to Rowan. "Come with me, up to the light."

Rowan and the others followed silently as he moved through the veil of water, up the stairs, and across the great empty room above. Without a sound, the doors swung open.

The space outside was crowded with people. Pandellis in blue. Umbray in silver. Fisk in green. All in their separate clans. They were staring out to sea, towards the rising sun.

The Keeper stepped out into the open air, the Crystal bright in his hands. A great cry went up. A cry of welcome, relief, and joy, as the people greeted him, and pointed to the sea.

Slowly the Keeper turned, and looked. The horizon was brown with Zebak sails. Rowan felt a chill of dread.

The Keeper held the Crystal high. It flashed like a beacon in the rising sun. The people's cries of joy became groans of fear as the brown sails leaped forward, as if in answer to a signal.

"He has called them in. We are lost," whispered Perlain.

The Keeper stood watching as the Zebak fleet flew towards them, swept before the wind. He made no move or sign.

Rowan felt a touch on his arm. "Take your mother," Jonn murmured in his ear. "Slip away through the crowd. Go as fast as you can, to Rin."

"I will not leave you, Jonn," said Jiller, overhearing.

"You must," he said grimly. "Someone must warn the people at home, so they are not taken by surprise."

"Then Rowan must go alone," she said. "I am still too weak to travel far. I would hold him back."

"Jiller, you must go!"

"I will not."

The people of Maris were deathly silent. All eyes were fixed on the Keeper. Waiting for his signal. Waiting for the order that would lead them to battle.

But the Keeper did not move.

I have done this, thought Rowan. And in the midst of his despair, he thought of Star, locked in her stable. Unable to run or defend herself. Waiting for slaughter at cruel hands.

He ran to the Keeper's side. "Doss—" he began. But the words died in his mouth as the Keeper turned to him.

"Doss of Pandellis is no more, Rowan of Rin," the Keeper said. "I am the Keeper of the Crystal."

"I thought—" Rowan began again. And again he broke off.

"You were right," said the Keeper softly, as if Rowan

had spoken his thought aloud. "Only wait."

The first Zebak ships were so close now that Rowan could see the cruel, triumphant faces of the warriors who lined the decks. He could see the black line that marked each forehead from nose to hairline. He could see the gleaming metal of their weapons.

The Keeper raised his arms. "Now!" he said quietly. The Crystal flashed, blinding.

And at that instant, great black clouds swept across the horizon. They tumbled thick and dark across the sky, driven before an ice-cold wind, smothering the sun, smothering the pale sky. The whole world dimmed, and became dark as night.

"What is happening?" cried Jonn. He grabbed Rowan's arm. "Rowan—"

The Keeper held the Crystal higher. There was a crash of thunder, and lightning split the sky, spearing into the white-capped water.

The people screamed. And on the sea the ships of the Zebak, trapped close together, spun and floundered. Masts broke and sails ripped as wind roared and lightning cracked around them.

Then there was a writhing and bubbling from the sea, and the water foamed as the twisting, coiling serpents of the deep rose to the surface, angered at their waking.

They hissed and snatched at the great fighting ships that in the face of their rage were as frail as leaves in a running stream. Wood tore and splintered, useless weapons clashed and fell into the foam, and the doomed Zebak's terrified cries were lost in the roaring of the wind.

Rowan turned away. He tried to remember that these

were the enemies of his people. That they had been coming to bring pain and death to those he loved. Still, he could not watch their destruction.

But the Keeper of the Crystal stood and saw it all. And only when it had finished did he calm the storm.

23 – Farewells

They were going home. Going with the blessings of the Maris, with many gifts, with promises to return soon. They had stayed two more days in Maris, to allow Jiller and Rowan time to rest. But now all of them longed to be gone.

When all was ready for the journey, Rowan left the safe house, and walked alone to the Cavern of the Crystal. The doors opened for him. He walked slowly across the empty, circular upper room, and down the stairs.

Welcome.

The Cavern was bathed in glorious light. The Keeper sat in his chair, surrounded by rainbows.

"I have come to say goodbye," said Rowan.

"It is not goodbye. You know that I will always be with you, Rowan of Rin," said the Keeper. "As you will always be with me."

Rowan nodded. He had not talked about this to anyone, even Jiller. But over the past days he had slowly realised the truth. That moment when the power of the Crystal had flowed through him to Doss of Pandellis had changed him for ever.

The Keeper smiled. "I have memories of Rin, though I have never seen it," he said. "I see the slip-daisies blooming yellow on the hills. I hear the bukshah lowing in the fields. I feel soft earth under my hands, and take pleasure in the small things growing."

"And I feel myself slipping through water like a fish," said Rowan. "I feel cool, wet sand under my feet. I mend nets by oil-fires at night. I hear sea-birds shrieking and see flying fish skimming the waves under a dark blue sky."

"So we understand one another, as no two people of Maris and of Rin ever have," said the Keeper. "And when I tell you that because of what happened on the morning you named your Choice your family will never again suffer at the hands of the Maris, you will believe me."

"Yes," said Rowan. "I will."

"On my orders Perlain of Pandellis has told the people what happened between us," the Keeper said. "He told them that I was a secret enemy of Maris, a tool of the Zebak, before I joined with the Crystal. But they saw with their own eyes what happened when the Zebak came."

He smiled. "And so at last they understand. It does not matter which clan brings forth the Keeper. Nothing can stand against the power of the Crystal. Not love of family, or friends, or home. Not loyalty to a clan or a country. Not even the mind games of an enemy."

"I only understood it when I felt the power for myself," Rowan whispered. "Only then did I realise that no Keeper could ever betray the people of Maris."

He turned to go. "Farewell, Doss," he said.

"Farewell, my friend," said the Keeper of the Crystal.

* * *

Many people stood at the outskirts of Maris to speed them on their way. Asha, Seaborn and Perlain were among them.

"Goodbye, Chooser of Rin." Asha shook Rowan's hand gravely. "I—am grateful to you."

Rowan blinked, unsure of what to say.

"If I had been Keeper, I would have ordered out the boats when the Zebak attacked. Because that is what has always been done. We would have fought, as we have always done. We might have won, by the power of the Crystal, but many of us would have died. You made the right choice in Doss of Pandellis. His mind is new and fresh. He will be like the Keepers of old. Using the Crystal, adding to its power, instead of only taking from it. And so I thank you."

She stepped back, stern and calm as always.

Seaborn came next. With him was a tall woman in the green of Fisk, her face no longer tight and serious, but full of light and joy. Rowan recognised her as one of the three who had escorted him to the Cavern. The woman who had watched them from the shore, when they were on the Island.

"This is Imlay. We are to marry in the summer, when my wounds have healed," Seaborn told him. "Perhaps you will come to our wedding. We would like to see you there, friend. You, more than any."

Rowan nodded, smiling. At last he understood the look of relief he had seen on Seaborn's face when he was told that he would not be Keeper of the Crystal. Seaborn was a strong, brave man. He had bent his will to his duty. He had tried his best to be what his clan wanted. But, having failed, he was free to live his life as he had longed to do. He was free to breathe the fresh air, to see the sky, to marry the woman he loved.

Perlain was last to bid them farewell. He shook hands with Jiller, with Jonn, and with Rowan. But Rowan noticed with a secret smile that he kept well away from Star.

"You may have no wish to visit the shores of Maris again, Rowan," Perlain said, in his formal way. "But should you come, my home will always be yours."

"I will be back," said Rowan. He glanced at Seaborn and Imlay, who stood watching from a distance. "If only for a wedding in the summer," he added.

Perlain smiled, and bowed.

And then Rowan, Jonn, Jiller and Star turned away from the sea, and began to walk. They walked for many minutes without speaking.

The river wound off into the distance, losing itself in the soft green hills. There was a long journey ahead, but none of them regretted it.

They were safe. They were together. And every step was taking them closer to home.